THOMAS

Illustrated by

Lurking among the misty moors of Scotland was Hugo Gifford, a dreadful warlock. His black eyes glittered; there were little points of red light inside them. And strangest of all – he cast no shadow. Thomas had banished all the other witches and wizards, but how could he be rid of this one?

MOLLIE HUNTER

Thomas and the Warlock

A Magnet Book

First published in Great Britain 1967
by Blackie Children's Books
This Magnet edition published 1986
by Methuen Children's Books Ltd
11 New Fetter Lane, London EC4P 4EE
Copyright © 1967 Mollie Hunter McIlwraith
Printed and bound in Great Britain by
Anchor Brendon Ltd, Tiptree, Essex

ISBN 0 416 51770 6

With love to Euan and Lachlan

Contents

ONE

The Broken Trap

There are no witches in Scotland any more, they say, and for that matter of it, neither are there any wizards—or warlocks, as they call them there. And the reason for that, they say also, is not far to seek—if you happen to know the story of Thomas and the Warlock.

This Thomas Thomson—to give him his full name—was the blacksmith in a little village in the Lowlands of Scotland. And a big, handsome fellow he was, with curling black hair, shoulders as wide as a door, and great strong arms. He was also a proper rascal, for he was a born poacher and he was forever being brought up in front of the Sheriff and fined for poaching trout and pheasants and suchlike from the laird's estate.

Thomas himself made a great joke of it when this happened to him, for he was a cheerful man with a great sense of humor. Even the Sheriff laughed at the tall tales he would spin to account for his presence in the laird's woods, but Thomas' wife Janet never laughed at them.

She was a bonny young woman, Janet, little and fair-haired, and she was a good wife to Thomas for she had a kindly nature and she was very fond of him. However, she simply could not treat his poaching as a joke because she was very strict in her view of what was right and what was wrong. Poaching, she knew, was very wrong, and so she felt it a great disgrace on herself to have a husband who was always in trouble for doing just that.

"Ach, lassie, ye shouldna vex yourself over him. He's more daft than wicked," Thomas' mother always told her, she being eighty-one, eighty-two come her birthday, and wise enough to see there was no real harm in Thomas. Moreover, she enjoyed listening to his tall tales and she was just as fond of a tasty trout or a fat pheasant for her dinner as he was himself.

However, Janet kept her sour face over the poaching, and the minister, the Reverend Goudie, backed her up by calling into the smithy to lecture Thomas for his sins every time he was in trouble with the Sheriff.

Thomas would listen to the lecture meekly and at the end of it he would heave up a sigh from the depths of his stomach and say:

"Ye've made me see the error o' my ways, minister, and that's a fact. And so help me, I'll do my best to mend them!"

He looked so humble, standing there with his eyes cast down to hide the twinkle in them and his great shoulders drooping, that the Reverend Goudie's heart was always touched. He would go on his way thinking that this time his lecture had done the trick, but as soon as he was gone Thomas would turn to his son Alexander and say with a grin:

"The best time for a walk through the woods is when the moon's down, eh, Alexander?"

And Alexander, who was ten and who thought his father was the funniest as well as the cleverest man in the world, would join in the laughter that followed this and wish that he could go poaching too.

Thomas would never take him, however.

"Your job is to look after your mother and Granma Thomson and play with Maggie when I'm out on the ran-dan," he told Alexander. "And forbye, one poacher in a family's plenty."

Alexander was disgusted at this for he thought that his mother and Granma Thomson were old enough to take care of themselves, while his sister Maggie was only a year-old baby and so not worth playing with. However, there was nothing he could do about it for Thomas could be stern when he liked, and so matters might have gone on without any change for long enough if the old laird had not died suddenly and his son, the young laird, succeeded to the estate.

Thomas was in a fix when this happened for the young laird was not the easy-going man his father had been. The water-bailiffs on the river and the gamekeepers in the woods all got new orders to shoot on sight at anyone they fancied might be a poacher, and since Thomas had no fancy for a bullet in the leg, he had to make up his mind how he was going to meet this new order of things.

He had no intention of giving up the fun he got out of poaching, of course, and so he decided that the only thing to do was to go farther afield for his sport, into another estate on the next parish. There was a drawback to this idea, however, for over the parish boundary was witch-country.

Or so many people believed, and it was said that the castle beside the wood over the parish boundary line used to be the stronghold of Hugo Gifford, the most fearsome warlock Scotland had ever known. And moreover, it was whispered from time to time that Hugo Gifford had never died but, in some shape or another, still lived in or near his old haunts.

"If ye see a tall man in black that casts no shadow—that's Hugo Gifford!" people used to say.

Then they would tell the tale of how Hugo Gifford had gone to learn the Black Arts from the Devil himself, along with a number of others that fancied themselves as warlocks. The Devil's fee for his teaching, they said, was the last man to leave the room when the lessons ended, and so when the time came for all the new warlocks to leave, there was a mighty rush for the door.

Hugo Gifford, however, sauntered out as if he had all the time in the world. The Devil rushed up and grabbed him but Hugo Gifford just said calmly:

"There's a man behind me yet."

It was only his shadow, of course, but the Devil was deceived. He grabbed the shadow and Hugo Gifford got clean away.

"And that," Thomas explained to Alexander, "is why Hugo Gifford never cast a shadow. He had none to cast."

"He must have been a terrible great warlock to cheat the Devil like that," Alexander said. "Ye'll no be safe poachin' *his* wood, Da."

"Havers!" snorted Thomas. "Hugo Gifford's deid these long years!"

"They still ca' that wood 'the Warlock's Wood,'" Alexander pointed out, "and they do say that Hugo Gifford still walks there."

"Ach, that's only a tale for bairns and auld wifies!" Thomas chaffed him. "Anyway, I'm off there the next moonless night we get. But mind, hold your wheesht so far as your mother's concerned or she'll tie me doon to the bed sooner than let me go!"

And so Alexander kept quiet as he had been told to do, and Thomas made ready to go poaching in the witch-country over the parish boundary line.

When the next moonless night came round, he slipped quietly out of bed, blackened his face so that it wouldn't show up pale in the darkness, and went cautiously into the kitchen to collect all his snares and traps. Then he slipped out to the stable beside the smithy and saddled his brown mare Peggy. He tied pads of cloth round her hoofs so that they wouldn't make a sound; then he mounted her and walked her out of the stable and down the village street.

Once clear of the village, he put Peggy to a trot and headed for the parish boundary. He was chuckling to himself as he rode for he foresaw a fine night's sport ahead of him, and as for witches——

"Well," he said to himself, "if they are at their can-trips tonight, they will have to be nimble to catch *me,* for I have a trick or two up my sleeve that no witch has ever learned!"

The night was as dark as any poacher could have wished, and darkest of all in the heart of the big wood where Thomas stopped at last to set his snares. This suited him down to the ground, however, for he had eyes like a cat in the darkness. And quiet as a cat he was too, moving through the wood and sniffing the air to test where the pheasants were roosting on the low branches of trees or the hares lying in their forms.

The rustle of leaves and the occasional sleepy chirp of a small bird were all the sounds that the wood gave back to him as he worked, but once or twice he heard a strange, loud shrieking sound. The first time it came, it made the hairs rise on the back of his neck with fear, and Peggy, the mare, whinnied wildly and tried to break free from the tree she was tied to. Thomas rose up from the trap he had been setting and listened hard, but no other sound or movement followed the screeching. The second time it came, he stopped and listened again, but when the wood remained deserted and silent this time also, he decided that it must have been a screech owl he had heard.

"Steady, Thomas, steady!" he told himself. "A hoolet is nothing to be feared of!"

All the same, he remembered the owl is a witch's bird, and the thought made his fingers tremble just a little on the lines of his snares.

However, Thomas was not the sort of man to flinch from any purpose he had set himself. He finished laying the traps for the hares and the snares for the roosting pheasants, and then he decided he would fill in the time of waiting till they were sprung by going to take a look at Hugo Gifford's castle.

"A cat may look at a king, after all," he said to himself, brushing aside the thought that this might be a daring thing to do. And so, leaving Peggy where she was in case anything startled her into making a noise, he went off through the wood in the direction of the warlock's castle.

It stood on a small but steep rise of ground to the east of the wood and only a few dozen yards from the outermost line of trees. Three wide grassy tracks led away from it in three different directions. The first one wandered along the edges of the ploughed land and grazing fields of the farmland around till it came to the main traffic road to the big town. The second one led up to the rolling grassy slopes of the Lammermuir Hills to the south, and the third one led north till it came to the coast-line of the sea inlet called the Firth of Forth.

Thomas stood and looked at the tracks and at the castle itself. The outer walls were in ruins now, with great holes in them and chunks of masonry sticking up through the gaps like huge broken teeth in an open mouth. It was only the tall central tower that still stood as solid as it had been ever since Hugo Gifford had built it over the great underground hall from which he ruled.

The Goblin Ha'—or "hall," as English people would say—that was the name the local people had given the warlock's castle. For that great underground cavern below the tower, they said, had been carved out of the solid rock of the mound on which the castle stood—and how else could the warlock have managed such a task without the aid of witches or demons or goblins of some kind?

And so they took care to keep clear of the Goblin Ha' and of the three roads along which all the warlocks and witches of the country were said to come riding from town and mountain and sea to gather at Hugo Gifford's meetings.

The back of Thomas' neck grew sore with craning to look up toward the top of the tower. He rubbed it with his hand to ease the stiffness and was just about to turn away when he noticed a movement among the shapes he had taken to be a row of small battlements crowning the top of the tower. He stepped forward for a closer look, and suddenly the things that had looked like battlements rose into the air on a great lifting of soundless wings.

It was owls he had seen perched in a row on the top of the tower! They screeched, their voices tearing wild and harsh through the darkness, and swooped down on him. And he, remembering the strong hooked beaks of screech owls and the great gripping talons of them, turned and ran for his life back into the wood.

They were down on him before he reached the safety of the trees, but he snatched off his jacket as he ran, and flailing it around his head with his strong blacksmith's arms, he managed to keep them at bay.

In among the trees he plunged and the owls followed him, but now their line of flight was broken by the tree trunks and the tall undergrowth between. One by one they dropped out of sight, and by the time Thomas reached the place where he had left Peggy tied, the pursuit was ended.

Thomas sank to the ground beside the mare, shaking and wiping the sweat off his face, and hardly able to believe what had happened. "Something gey queer must have got into they hoolets," he thought, for never in all his born days had he heard of owls attacking a man, and he shivered again, wondering if the owls were the warlock's creatures sent purposely to attack him for having ventured too close to the Goblin Ha'.

Peggy stamped and whinnied uneasily by his side and at last he got to his feet, put on his jacket, and spent some minutes calming her down before he set off to examine his traps. Daylight was not far off, and so it was time to see what they held and then head for home.

It was a rich haul he had got—hares and rabbits, and a brace of pheasants that had come down from their

perches to examine the corn he had scattered round their snares. He stuffed each one into the deep poacher's pockets inside his jacket as he worked his way back along the trap-line to the place where he had left Peggy, but he was still a hundred yards from her when he heard her give a great whicker of alarm.

The sound of something heavy crashing about in the undergrowth followed hard on the mare's call, but Thomas did not stop to think what this might be. He took to his heels and ran like the wind to save Peggy from whatever danger had made her give that cry of terror.

She was still stamping and prancing about when he came in sight of her, but there was no sign of the person or thing, whatever it was, that had alarmed her. The only unusual thing Thomas could see was one of his own traps, of the sort he used for hares, lying broken almost in two pieces on the path in front of the mare.

He looked at the trap, turned it over with his foot, and then bent down to have a closer look at it. Something had been caught in it. There were specks of blood on it and small tufts of gray fur caught between the wires. Carefully Thomas examined the fur. A hare's fur—that's what it was. There had been a hare caught in the trap and somehow it had managed to break loose from it. But how? A full-grown hare could be a powerful creature, but this was a strong trap.

Thomas looked from the fur to the mare. She was still turning restlessly about the rope that tied her, the whites of her eyes were showing as she rolled them, and her ears were laid flat back against her head. Clearly, Peggy had been terrified by the creature that had broken out of the trap, and as Thomas realized this, an awful thought suddenly crossed his mind.

Without any more ado he swept his traps together, unhitched Peggy, and mounted her and rode straight home as fast as he could go.

TWO

The Tall Stranger

Janet scolded her head off when she came downstairs that morning and found her larder hung with newly trapped game. Thomas, however, pretended to be very busy in the smithy and with all the noise he made, blowing up the big bellows that kept the fire in the forge roaring and the clang of his hammer on the anvil, Janet could hardly make herself heard. Which, of course, was exactly what Thomas had intended should happen.

When she came to the end of her scolding, he just said with a laugh, "Ye'll have a fine time at the stove, though, when ye come to cook a' that game. Will ye no, eh, Janet woman?"

And in this way he found Janet's weak spot for she was a rare cook and she could no more resist making a fine dinner than Thomas could resist catching game for the pot. So off she went to look up her recipes; Thomas got on with his work in earnest, and a few minutes later Alexander came running into the smithy.

He had just come from having a look in the larder too, and so he was in a high state of excitement and as full of questions as an egg is full of meat. It was question and answer all the way between him and Thomas to begin with, and then Thomas hushed him down so that he could tell the story of the events in the Warlock's Wood in his own way. When he came to the part about hearing Peggy cry out in terror, however, Alexander could hold his curiosity no longer and he broke in:

"Was it a witch that frightened her, Da? Did ye see a witch?"

"I *saw* no witch, laddie," Thomas told him, "but I did find this."

He put his hand into his pocket and drew out the tufts of hare fur he had found clinging to the broken trap. Then he held the fur out for Alexander to examine, and went on:

"I found this stuck to the wires of a trap that had been broken nearly in half, and there's no hare alive could have done *that*. But I have heard tell that witches can change their shapes at will. And of the different shapes they can take the two they like best are those of a cat— and a hare!"

"Why these two creatures more than any other?" Alexander asked.

"Think of the soundless way a cat can move," Thomas

pointed out. "Think of the turn of speed a hare can show!"

"But surely, Da," Alexander objected, "the witches ken the terrible risk they run of being caught in a trap while they're in such a shape."

"Oh, aye," agreed Thomas. "But it's nothing like the risk it would be for them to go about their wicked ways in their own shape! For instance, if a witch wanted to get into your house to work ye harm, what safer way would there be for her than to slip in at the door at night in the shape of a cat? Ye'd never think ill of a poor strange pussy, would ye? And if a warlock wanted to ruin a farmer's crops, what better way would there be to hide his true self while he cast his spell than to run through the corn in the shape of a hare? The farmer would chase a warlock for his life if he saw him striding about his fields, but he wouldna think to run and set a trap every time he saw a harmless creature like a hare in his corn."

And while Alexander thought this over he added, "And forbye, laddie, ye must remember there was naebody— the warlock included—that knew I would be setting traps in the Warlock's Wood last night. If there *were* witches about in the wood then, they must have thought they were fine and safe from such a chance."

"And was it—d'ye think it was a witch was caught in your trap?" Alexander whispered.

"It would take a wiser man than me to answer that," Thomas told him, and put the hare fur carefully back in his pocket. "But whatever it was that was held there would have needed more than a hare's strength to break free. Forbye, it frightened Peggy half to death, and I've never seen her take fright at a hare before."

The two of them looked solemnly at one another and then Alexander asked:

"D'ye think we'll ever ken what happened, Da?"

"Maybe aye, maybe no," Thomas said cautiously. "But remember—there was blood on the trap. Whatever or whoever was caught in it will likely be lame for a while, so you keep your eyes open, son, and if ye see a limping woman come quickly and tell either me or Granma Thomson. Or a man, of course! It could as easy be a warlock as a witch that was caught in the trap."

"But ye'll not go to the Warlock's Wood again, will ye, Da?" Alexander asked. "Ye'll no risk *that* again, surely."

He spoke very earnestly for the idea of his father in danger from witchcraft frightened him. Thomas, however, wasn't too keen to give a straight yes or no for an answer, especially since he had suffered no harm for all the strangeness of his adventure in the wood.

"We'll see," he said. "We'll see. I'm back safe and sound in my own smithy, after all, am I no?"

Still Alexander looked doubtful, but the school bell began to ring at that minute and so Thomas had a good excuse for chasing him away out of the smithy.

"See now ye put this out of your mind and pay attention to your lessons!" he shouted after him, and went back to his anvil whistling cheerfully to himself. It had been no such great risk to take, after all, to go into the Warlock's Wood—and better a few daft owls chasing him than a gang of gamekeepers ready to put a bullet into his leg!

He *would* go back there again, he thought—and to blazes with Hugo Gifford! And with that decision he picked up his hammer and started work again, chuckling as he thought of the expression on the laird's face when he heard that Thomas Thomson had got himself a bag of game again in spite of all the new measures that had been taken to keep him from poaching. And this time he had a tale to tell that needed no embroidery on the truth!

Now game needs to be hung for a few days before it is tender enough to cook, and so Thomas had plenty of time to tell his adventure in the wood to the rest of the men in the village. Plenty of opportunity too, for it was always at the smithy that the men of the village gathered to exchange news and talk about the weather and the crops.

First one and then another would stop by the smithy door of an evening and pass the time of day with Thomas, and gradually a little crowd would collect there. In the winter, it was snugly round the fire in the forge they gathered to talk, and in the summer, it was outside in the smithy yard they sat basking in the evening sun.

Pipes would be pulled out and lit up and a jar of beer passed around, and while the brown beer flowed and the blue smoke drifted, the talk would flow and drift with them. Tall tales were told in plenty then and many a strange story spun—most of all when it was Thomas himself that held the floor with one of his poaching yarns.

So it was like this, then, that he told the story of his adventure in the Warlock's Wood, and being Thomas, of course, he made a great joke of it. And being Thomas, nobody believed a word of the tale!

It was just another story made up for their amusement, they decided, and Thomas was too good-natured to argue them out of this belief. Besides, he didn't want to spoil the joke by insisting how scared he really had been at the time it all happened.

Alexander and Granma Thomson were the only two who took the matter seriously, and for once Granma Thomson was as angry with Thomas as Janet was.

"Ye'll get more than ye bargain for if ye laugh at such things, Thomas," she warned and kept on warning him, but Thomas only shrugged and laughed and kept on telling his story.

It wasn't long, of course, before the news that he had been poaching again got round to the laird and to the minister, too. The pair of them met to discuss the stories they had heard and eventually they decided they would go to Thomas' house and have the matter out with the rascal, once and for all.

Down the village street they came together, and as it happened, it was just the day when Janet was preparing a big, fine dinner of the spoils that they chose to arrive at Thomas' house. The smell of the dinner cooking came wafting to them out of the open door. They stopped, their heads lifted and their noses twitching like a pair of hounds on a breast-high scent and then, without waiting to exchange a word with one another or even to knock on the door, the pair of them plunged into the house and burst angrily into the kitchen.

Janet was standing at the stove. Alexander and Granma Thomson were sitting one on either side of the table, and Thomas sat at the head of it with Maggie in her cradle beside his chair. The table was spread with a fine white cloth and set for dinner, and the load on it made the laird's and the minister's eyes stand out on stalks.

A great tureen of hare soup steamed, rich and brown, in the middle of the table. On one side of this was a big round game pie, with a little wisp of savory steam escaping from the hole in the center of its thick, flaky crust of pastry. On a dish beside the pie lay two plump, golden-brown pheasants, and beside them a great pie dish heaped with gleaming, freshly buttered potatoes.

Alexander had his soup spoon up ready in his hand. Granma Thomson had just taken the lid off the soup tureen. Thomas was whistling and sharpening the carving knife as he whistled. The three of them looked up and Janet swung round from the stove as the laird and the minister burst in, and everybody stared at everybody else for a second. Then the laird and the minister found their tongues.

"Oh, you rascal, Thomas Thomson, I'll have you hanged!" the laird shouted, quite beside himself with rage for the moment; and the minister cried in the same breath, "Thomas Thomson, you are the greatest and wickedest sinner on earth!"

"That's right—ye're both right!" wailed Janet. "And I'm as bad as he is, sirs, for the vanity that led me to cook such a fine dinner out of his ill-gotten gains!"

With that she sat down in her place at the table and put her pretty fair head down beside the dish of buttered potatoes and wept for shame at both herself and Thomas. He, however, rose up as she sat down and said cheerfully:

"Now laird and minister, ye have me wrong for once, for the dinner ye see here never ran about in the laird's woods! So sit you down, the both of you. Alexander, you set places for the gentlemen and they can join us while I tell the story of how we came by all this."

"I'll not touch a bite!" the laird said angrily.

"It would choke me!" the minister chimed in.

"Ach, that's foolish," Thomas told them. "There's plenty for all, and there's no sense in wasting good food."

He waved his hand round the tempting display of food on the table. The laird and the minister both felt their mouths watering and swallowed hard. They glanced at one another and looked away again, greed struggling now with the wrath in their hearts. Janet looked up and when she saw the expressions on their faces she repeated hopefully:

"There *is* no sense in wasting good food, sirs."

"It's dinner time too, and ye'll both be hungry," Granma Thomson coaxed.

"Aye, we are, and waste *is* wicked," agreed the minister doubtfully, feeling the delicious smell of the hare soup tickle his nostrils.

The laird, with his eye on the golden-brown pheasants, said ungraciously:

"Well, I wouldn't want to insult your good cooking by refusing to taste it, mistress."

"That's settled, then," Thomas said briskly. "Pull up your chairs, gentlemen. Janet, wipe your eyes. And Granma, you get on with the serving."

The laird and the minister sat down at the places Alexander had set for them, both still trying to keep up a pretense of doing so only for good manners' sake. Janet dried her eyes. Granma Thomson ladled out the soup, and when this had been supped, Thomas carved the game pie and then the pheasants.

For a while there was no sound but the champing of jaws and the clink of knives and forks for everyone was too intent on the meal to have time for conversation. When the last pheasant bone had been picked, however, and Alexander had speared the last of the buttered potatoes onto his plate, Thomas sat back and prepared to talk. He loosened his belt and lit up his pipe. Janet and Granma Thomson went off to the scullery to wash the dishes, and when they had gone, he told the laird and the minister the story of his expedition to the Warlock's Wood.

He spoke seriously enough for him this time for, although he enjoyed the thought of scoring over the laird, he knew he had to convince him he was telling the truth or be brought up in front of the Sheriff again. Furthermore, it struck him that, since the Powers of Darkness had been up to their tricks, the Reverend Goudie might well want to warn his brother-minister in the next parish about it.

As soon as he was finished speaking, however, the laird said, "I don't believe a word of that nonsense, Thomas Thomson. You got that game in my woods and I'll have you up before the Sheriff for it!"

Thomas rose up and lifted a trap from among a pile lying in a corner. He held it out to the laird.

"Is there any creature in your woods could break a trap the way that one is broken?"

The laird looked closely at the trap and a puzzled frown came over his face. Thomas turned to the minister.

"Do *you* believe me, minister?"

"I do not," said the minister promptly, "for I know very well you are a stranger to the truth! But if you *did* go poaching in the Warlock's Wood, Thomas, and if you *did* by chance catch a witch in one of your traps—then beware, man, for you have meddled in strange and wicked matters and you may pay for it with your soul in the end!"

Thomas had no time to reply to this stern warning for at this moment Alexander, who had run out of the house as soon as he had eaten his last mouthful, came bursting in again and cried:

"Da, ye're wanted at the smithy. There's a gentleman with a horse and trap askin' for you."

Thomas excused himself to the other two and went out to the smithy, and there he found the horse and trap standing by the smithy door, and the gentleman Alexander had mentioned waiting for him inside the smithy.

The fire in the forge was low and so there was not much light in the smithy, but there was enough for Thomas to see that his customer was a tall man dressed in an elegant black suit with a tall black hat on his head. His face was nowhere near as handsome as his clothes, however, for it was long and narrow with a great nose as sharp as an eagle's beak. His eyes were a bit out of the ordinary too, for they were so black that they looked like two polished ovals of ebony and they glittered strangely with little points of red light as he looked at Thomas.

However, Thomas decided uneasily, the glitter might well be due to some trick of light reflecting from the fire in the forge, and he listened politely as the stranger said:

"I need your skill, smith. Can you put a new iron rim on one of the wheels of my trap?"

"Easy, sir. No bother," Thomas said, quite relieved to find such a simple demand being made of him. "I'll take a look at the trap for you right away."

He went outside again and examined the trap. The wheels were of wood with the rim bound by a broad hoop of iron, as was common in those times, and although the iron band round one wheel was sound and smooth, the iron on the other was all chipped and worn round the edges. The trap itself was a very smart little carriage of polished black wood with the panels trimmed in silver. The leather seats were black also, and on one of them lay a bridle and a black, silver-trimmed saddle.

The stranger, who had followed Thomas out to the trap, caught the glance he gave at this saddle and said:

"Unharness the horse then, smith, and drop that saddle over its back. I shall leave the trap with you meantime."

"Aye, sir," said Thomas, and went to do as he was bid. The horse, which was as black and shining as the trap itself, flattened its ears and jerked its head back from his reaching hand. Its long upper lip snickered back over its teeth. A quiver ran over its whole body, and Thomas—who knew a vicious horse when he saw one—drew his hand sharply back again.

The stranger spoke several words that could have been double Dutch for all that Thomas could guess of their meaning, and the horse's quivering body was suddenly still again. Its head drooped slowly down and it stood as meek and quiet as any old plow horse while Thomas unharnessed it from the trap, led it out from between the shafts, and saddled it with the black and silver saddle.

The tall stranger swung up onto its back. Thomas looked up at him and asked:

"When will ye be needin' the trap then, sir?"

"That depends," the stranger answered, eyeing him—as Thomas thought—rather oddly.

"On what, sir?" he asked, puzzled.

"On yourself—does it not?"

"Oh, aye." Thomas looked round at all the broken plowshares and other work in hand stacked neatly against the smithy wall. The stranger must have realized how busy he was, thought he, and was leaving him to choose his own time for the business of mending the wheel.

"I'll have it ready as soon as I can, sir," he promised. "And what name shall I put on the bill for the work?"

"Gifford," the stranger said. "H. Gifford."

With a little flick of the reins, he turned the horse and rode rapidly out of the smithy yard. Thomas stood staring after him with his mind so far away that he never noticed the minister and the laird and Alexander coming up to stand beside him. The laird jogged his elbow. Thomas came to himself with a start and looked from one to the other of the two men and then down at Alexander. They all stared back at him in silence and at last he asked in a choking voice:

"Did ye hear what he called himself?"

"We heard," the laird told him grimly; and the minister asked, "Thomas, did you notice anything unusual about him when he walked out of the smithy into the yard, here?"

Thomas shook his head. "I didna see him then. He came out behind me."

The minister turned to the laird. "Laird, did *you* notice anything unusual about him?"

"He limped," the laird said promptly, and Alexander chimed in:

"He did, Da. I saw him plain. He was lame in the one foot."

There was a long silence. The minister looked up toward the sun standing high in the sky and then his eyes came down to study the dark shadows it was casting.

"There was one other thing about him, Thomas," he said quietly. "He cast no shadow—no shadow at all."

THREE

The Wheel

Neither Thomas nor the laird, nor yet the minister knew quite what to make of this strange incident, not even after they had argued all the ins and outs of it for an hour among themselves.

The only conclusions the laird and the minister came to were that they must hold their judgment on Thomas' story for the time being, and that Thomas himself had better watch his step in future. And they agreed with him that it would be wiser not to tell Janet meanwhile about the tall stranger's visit.

For said Thomas, "She's easy vexed, is Janet. And she would be sore vexed indeed if she knew what we think we know this day."

There was no harm in telling Granma Thomson, however, since she was too wise and tough and old to be frightened by anything living. And besides, Thomas

wanted her advice on the matter, for although he had no
fear of any danger the Warlock's ill-will might bring on
himself, he was a little afraid on behalf of Alexander and
Maggie.

"Ye have the heart of the matter there, Thomas,"
Granma Thomson said when he told her this. "We must
keep the bairns safe at all costs, and I'm just the body
that can show you how to do that!"

Off she went then and rummaged in a big wooden box
she kept under her bed, and when she came back she had
two little things like lockets in her hand. They were
pieces of pink coral set in silver and each one was hung
on a little silver chain. She put one round the baby Maggie's neck, and she would have hung the other round
Alexander's neck but he would have none of it.

"I dinna *want* to wear it," objected he. "It's only lass-
ies that wear things like that!"

Granma Thomson was annoyed with him. "This is a
sure charm against witchcraft," she told him angrily,
"and ye'll maybe rue the day if ye dinna wear it."

Alexander was stubborn, however, and Thomas
backed him up for he could see that it would be an affront
to a boy's pride to wear a charm round his neck like a
girl.

"I'll tell ye what, Granma Thomson," he said. "I'll
take a branch of a rowan tree and nail it to the lintel over
the door. There's no witch can come into a house pro-
tected by rowan wood, and so that will take care of us all
—Alexander included."

Granma Thomson was content with this and Alexander was pleased for, although he was unwilling to wear the charm, he did want some sort of protection against the warlock. It was a different matter altogether with Janet, however, when she saw the rowan wood nailed over the door and found the charm round Maggie's neck.

"They're downright heathen things, Thomas Thomson," she raged, "and I'm black affronted to have a charm against witchcraft over my door and another one round my bairn's neck. So you just put them back where they came from!"

"They're fine where they are, mistress," Thomas insisted, "so just you let them stay, even if it is only a foolish fancy of mine to have them there."

Still Janet argued and grumbled, although she didn't quite dare to go straight against Thomas and put the charms away. So it went on for more than a week after the tall stranger's visit, and then one day Thomas got tired of all the argy-bargy over the charms.

"Woman, I'll be master in my own house!" he roared at Janet. "The charms will stay and that's an end of it, so not another word from you on the subject."

Out he went then to the smithy with the determined look still on his face, for the argument with Janet over the charms had made up his mind for him on quite a different matter—and that was the question of whether he should or should not put a new rim on the wheel of the stranger's trap.

For if their fears were right and the stranger, H. Gifford, really was Hugo Gifford, the warlock, would he not simply be helping him about his unholy business by repairing the wheel? On the other hand, he himself had not seen the stranger limping nor had he noticed that he had no shadow. Supposing it was only his tale of the events in the Warlock's Wood that had led Alexander and the minister and the laird to imagine these things?

If that was so and the stranger was *not* Hugo Gifford, he would simply think that the work had been left undone because of some failure in his craftsman's skill—an idea that hurt Thomas' pride more than anything in the world could have done!

So Thomas had been arguing with himself for the past week, but now the question was settled in his mind. He *would* mend the wheel and defy the stranger, or Hugo Gifford, or any other person for that matter of it, to do their worst. Let Janet scold about the charms and Granma warn to her heart's content about the danger of dealing with a warlock, he would still show them and everyone else that Thomas Thomson was master in his own house. And a master of his craft forbye, he thought to himself, gazing at the broken rim of the wheel and seeing in his mind's eye the skillful job he could make of repairing it.

"Alexander!" he shouted. "Run you and gather all the laddies with their watering cans. I'm goin' to mend this wheel."

Alexander gave a skirl of delight and darted off down

the village street, knocking on doors, calling down garden paths, and gradually gathering behind him a long
tail of boys all armed with big watering cans and all
shouting with delight like himself.

When the last boy was rounded up, they all marched
back up to the smithy, filled their watering cans and
stood them around the outer edge of a flat, circular plate
of iron let into the ground of the smithy yard and lying
level with it.

A circular hole in the middle of this flat plate was
meant to contain the hub of the wheel, so allowing the
spokes of it to lie level and steady on the plate while the
new rim was being fixed on. The wheel of the stranger's
trap was already lying in this position by the time the
boys arrived, and so, as soon as the watering cans had
been placed in readiness round it, they all crowded into
the smithy to watch the next stage in the operation.

Alexander was in the forefront of this rush into the
smithy for he knew that the first boy in would be told to
work the big bellows that blew up the fire in the forge,
and of all the jobs he was accustomed to doing in the
smithy, this was the one he enjoyed most.

Thomas already had the fire stoked in the great stone
forge that ran like a wide shelf right across one side of
the smithy. The new rim for the wheel lay propped
against the bigger of his two anvils, and he had pincers
for grasping it ready in his hand.

"Blow her up, lad!" he roared to Alexander, and Alex-

ander ran to the huge leather bellows that stood, nearly
the height of a man, beside the forge. He leaped to grasp
the long wooden handle sticking out of the top of the bellows. His hands closed over it and his weight brought the
handle swinging down. The bellows wheezed like a giant
clearing its throat; then as Alexander pumped at the
handle, the great leather bag of it filled with air. Up and
down he pumped at the handle, in and out the bellows
breathed its great breath into the forge till suddenly the
red glow of the heaped coals there burst into roaring
golden flame.

The boys cheered. Alexander's strokes on the handle
grew so long and strong that he was lifted right off his
feet with the upward swing of it. Another two boys
leaped to his aid, and like three mad monkeys swinging
from the handle, they pumped furiously at the bellows.

When they were tired, another three boys eagerly took
over from them, and Alexander sat down on the smaller
of the anvils to watch the iron rim for the wheel being
thrust into the fire.

Thomas gripped it firmly with his pincers, swung it
round and up, and thrust it straight into the heart of the
huge fire blazing in the forge. There was a "whoosh" like
a rocket going up, and the fire exploded upwards into the
enormous black throat of the forge's chimney.

Thomas still had a grip of the iron circle with his pincers and now slowly, very slowly, he began to turn it
round and round inside the heart of the fire so that every

bit of it would receive an even heat. Each time he moved the wheel a little, a fresh stream of sparks shot up from the fire and raced in a crackling stream of red and gold up the yawning blackness of the chimney's throat.

The iron rim began to glow a dull red with the heat, the dull red changed slowly to an almost transparent rose-pink, and as the heat grew more and more intense, the rose-pink color began to fade away to nothing for now the iron was becoming white-hot.

Still Thomas crouched in front of the fire, holding the wheel steady and turning it with his pincers. His face shone in the light of the fire with the great beads of sweat that started out on his forehead and trickled downwards; the muscles of his strong brown arms bulged and strained with the effort of holding the iron steady, but not for one second did he relax his grip on the pincers or budge back an inch from the heat of the fire.

The flames of it lit the rest of the smithy with a deep, ruddy glow. They set a weird dance of flickering light and shadow going high up among the beams and rafters of the ceiling, and they glowed in points of golden light on the polished hafts of the anvils and the blades of the tools hanging in their racks on the walls.

They darted out at Thomas, and Alexander watched him fearfully for the flames were so close to him that they seemed almost to lick him with their fiery tongues. Still Thomas stood rock-steady among them and held firmly onto the white-hot metal, and Alexander's fear

turned to a great sense of wonder for now he could sense something more in his father than the strength that made his muscles bulge and the courage that would not let him flinch back from the heat of the fire.

There was pride flowing out of Thomas—pride in the power he had over the hard strength of the iron. For now he was overcoming that hard strength. Now he was taming it in the fire, making it soft and yielding so that when the moment came to shape it, the iron would be his servant and he would be the master of the iron.

That was a great thing, thought Alexander—to be the master of so hard and strong a thing as iron! And he thought to himself, no wonder his father was proud! A blacksmith has a right to be proud of his craft.

The entire circle of iron was now white-hot. Thomas threw a quick glance behind him and roared:

"Stand by with the watering cans!"

The boys scattered from their places in the smithy and rushed outside. Each one grabbed a can of water. Thomas planted his feet well apart, braced his shoulders, and with one mighty heave he lifted the iron rim clear of the fire. His teeth gleaming white in a grin of effort and his hands on the pincers all veined and knotted with the strength of their grip, he swung the rim round to face the door and marched with it held high in front of him into the smithy yard.

As the colder air outside the smithy touched it, its heat dropped suddenly from white-hot to red-hot. For a split second Alexander glimpsed it above him, a great blood-red circle suspended in the air and held clear of him only by the power of his father's arms. Then Thomas swung it downwards in one quick, skillful movement that fitted it neatly into place round the wooden wheel of the trap.

In the second that the red-hot iron rim slid into place around the wooden wheel, each boy tilted his watering can and played a cooling stream over the iron. A tremendous hissing sound arose as the water touched the hot iron and turned immediately to steam. Wheel, black-smith, and boys together disappeared from view in the midst of a great cloud of this steam, but still the boys kept pouring, moving round and round the wheel in a shuffling circle so that Thomas could move with them, tap-tapping the rim firmly into position on the wheel as he went.

The water began to run low in the cans, and now the excitement spread outward from its center in the heart of the cloud of steam as boy after boy darted from the wheel to the tap in the smithy wall to refill his can, and then rushed, yelling triumphantly, back into the steam.

Alexander rushed for fresh water in his turn, and looking back over his shoulder as he waited impatiently for his can to fill, he saw that the first great cloud of steam was begining to drift and break up. He could see faces appearing here and there through the breaks in it, and the forms of boys bobbing wildly up and down in the cloud like hobgoblins dancing in mist.

At odd seconds, he glimpsed Thomas bent double as he shuffled rapidly round tapping at the wheel and then, just as he snatched up his can to run back to the wheel, he saw a stranger's face looming up suddenly through the steam. It seemed to rise right out of the midst of the cloud, but he knew that was impossible for the face was a woman's one. And no woman ever took part in the business of dousing the wheel!

For a second, Alexander hesitated where he stood for there had been something odd and unusual about the strange woman's face, and a little shiver of fear ran over him at the sight of it. However, the steam hid it from view again almost immediately, and so he shook off the feeling and rushed back to the wheel to continue pouring with the rest of the boys.

He had circled the wheel again a few times when he realized that there really was a strange woman standing near it and that he *had* glimpsed her face—although he must have imagined he had seen it appearing in the middle of the steam instead of at the edge of it.

Each time after that when he passed in front of the point where she was standing, he glanced again at her. She stood perfectly still, patiently watching the hurly-burly round the wheel, and it was clear that she was waiting for something.

But what? Alexander wondered. She seemed very intent on what was going on, and yet women were not usually interested in the work of the smithy. And what was it about her that had seemed so odd to him when he had first glimpsed her?

He was still wondering about the woman by the time the work on the wheel was finished and Thomas was standing leaning on his hammer and wiping the sweat from his brow. Alexander tugged gently at his leather apron to draw his attention, and with a nod of his head in the woman's direction, he whispered:

"Who's yon bonny lass, Da?"

Thomas looked down at him and then across at the woman, and he laughed. "I doubt ye're no seein' straight yet, laddie, after a' that steam in your eyes. Yon's no a lassie! She's as wrinkled-lookin' an auld wife as ever I saw!"

Before Alexander could answer this, the woman moved toward them. Thomas gave her good-day and she gave him a civil reply. Then she looked down at the finished wheel and she said:

"It seems you are every bit as good a smith as I have heard tell, sir."

"I take a pride in my craft, mistress," Thomas told her politely, and as politely in her turn she replied:

"And so I will take care to tell to those who may need a smith's work."

And then she added, "As I do now."

"We'll talk business then, mistress," Thomas said, and then to Alexander's disappointment, he told him:

"Run you in to your mother and say I'll be a wee while yet till I come in for my dinner."

Alexander went, with a curious backward glance at the strange woman, but she—as if she was afraid of his searching look, turned her face sharply away from him so that he could not see whether she was as young as he thought she was or as old as his father had said she was.

FOUR

The Iron Pot

"She wanted me to make her a pot—an iron pot," Thomas said later on when Alexander asked him what the strange woman's business had been. "I told her I could do it but I'm gey busy just now and she would have to wait for it, and so she's comin' back in a week's time."

"Why did ye say she was old, Da?" Alexander asked. "I saw her clear and she was young an' bonny."

Thomas was in nothing like his usual good humor by this time for the hard work on the wheel had tired him. Moreover, his conscience was troubling him over having been so stern with Janet, and he was not so sure now that he ought to have done the work on the wheel at all.

"If your eyes are as bad as all that, laddie," he told Alexander shortly, "it's early to bed for a few nights and a dose of senna ye need. That'll stop your eyes playing tricks on you!"

"Aye, Da," said Alexander meekly, and slipped quickly out of the house, for there was no worse-tasting medicine than senna in his view and he was afraid his mother would decide that he would be the better of a dose of it anyway!

He would take another good look at the strange woman when she called for her pot, he decided, and then he would know for sure whether or not his eyes had been playing tricks on him and what it was about the woman's face he had glimpsed so oddly through the clouds of steam.

Thomas watched him go and sighed to think he had been so short with him. It might be better after all to give the poaching a rest, he thought—at least until he knew one way or another whether the tall stranger really had been Hugo Gifford the warlock. Besides, it was wearing on to spring. In a week or so, the birds would be nesting and the hares lying up in their forms. The end of the poaching season was in sight for the time being and he was busy in the smithy in any case.

So Thomas decided to follow the laird's and the minister's advice and tread cautiously for a while. He kept his head down at work in the smithy, went early to bed and slept soundly, and never took so much as a look at his traps. And by the end of the first week of this kind of life, he had got through as much work as he usually did in three weeks of the poaching season.

The old woman's iron pot was made and placed on a

shelf ready to be collected. Alexander said nothing more to him of the strange notion he had had about her, and Thomas decided it must have been just one of those fancies that children are always making up in their heads. He thought nothing of it, therefore, when Alexander appeared in the smithy on the day the old woman came to collect her pot and so he did not notice how hard Alexander was staring at her.

The woman noticed it, however, and as soon as she did so, she turned her face sharply away from Alexander. Thomas went over to the shelf where the pot stood, and Alexander moved slightly so that he could get a good view of the woman's face again.

From this new angle he saw her as he had first glimpsed her through the steam, and the same little shiver ran through him for now he could see the same odd thing about her that he had noticed then. Her face was neither young nor old, but both at the same time. The features of it blurred and quivered under his eyes as they had seemed to blur and quiver within the clouds of steam, so that he could not see clearly what they were like.

It was only when he stared hard at her, as he had done after the wheel was mended and as he was doing now, that her face suddenly seemed to become that of a bonny young woman, and he was just going to turn and whisper this to his father when the woman shot him a warning glance that froze the words on his lips. Thomas came

across to them at that moment with the pot in his hand,
and the old woman began to fumble for the money to pay
him.

Her purse seemed to be hidden somewhere in the folds
of the long ragged gown she wore, and her fingers were
stiff and slow in finding it. When she got it out at last,
the clasp was stiff. She had a struggle to open it, and
Alexander could see his father watching her with a mix-
ture of pity and impatience on his good-natured face.

The old woman got the purse open at last and began
to grope inside it. Her fingers shook as she fumbled to
bring out the coins there. She sighed and muttered all the
time as if she was afraid she would not have enough to
pay for the pot, so that Alexander felt sorry for her being
so poor and would have liked to whisper to his father to
let her have the pot for nothing. He glanced at Thomas
and saw that he was feeling the same way, and so he was
delighted when the old woman held out the coins at last
and his father said gently:

"Keep your money, mistress. I get few orders for pots
in the ordinary way and so it was a pleasure to try my
hand at casting this one for you."

"Well—thank you kindly, smith," the old woman said
uncertainly. Then, with an odd little look at Thomas, she
added, "—though I think I have as much here as would
pay for it."

"Oh, aye, I see that fine," Thomas said quickly, not
wanting her to realize he could see how poor she was.

"But ye'll no deny me the pleasure o' givin' now, surely?"

"No—no, indeed," said she, still looking at him with that odd expression on her face. "I'll take it as kindly as it was meant, and remember you always with thanks."

"Fine, fine!" Thomas said. "And Alexander here will carry it home for you, mistress."

"No need for that," the old woman said hastily. "It's a heavy pot for a wee boy to carry."

"It's heavier for the like of yourself, wifie," Thomas told her, "and Alexander is a strong boy and willing. You let him carry it and ye'll be back beside your own hearth in half the time."

With that, he handed the pot to Alexander and gave him a little push out of the door with it. The old woman frowned and muttered something, but she fell into step with Alexander all the same and walked with him down the village street. When they came to the end of the street, she took the path that ran past the wall of the laird's estate. Then she branched off onto a track that Alexander thought must lead to the Lammermuir Hills, although he had never been there before. The countryside around it was rough with coarse grass and heather and bracken and great patches of gorse bushes, and he followed her wondering how far off her house was and where it lay. However, the old woman kept in front of him all the way. She walked quickly and in silence and he was too shy to ask her any questions.

They had been walking like this for more than an hour when the old woman stopped and turned to him. She reached out a hand for the pot and said roughly:

"Be off with you now, boy. I will manage from here by myself."

Alexander looked at her in surprise. "My da said I was to carry it home for you, mistress," he protested, but she swung the pot out of his hand without another word and walked on rapidly by herself.

Alexander watched her till a dip in the path hid her from his sight. He was hurt by the rough way she had spoken to him, and also he was puzzled to know why she was so unwilling to let him help her. It was strange, he thought, and wondered if her manner had anything to do with the warning look she had shot him in the smithy.

Why *had* she looked at him like that? Was it because she knew he was seeing her differently from the way his father saw her and was warning him to keep quiet about it? Was it because she knew he saw her differently that she was so unwilling to let him walk home with her? What was she trying to hide from him?

A great curiosity to find the answer to all these questions suddenly gripped Alexander. Quickly he walked on in the direction the old woman had taken, and beyond the dip in the path he saw her again.

She was still walking at the same rapid pace, swinging the pot in her hand, and after a moment he began cautiously to follow her.

By this time the path had become only a rough, nar-

row track winding between great boulders and round big
stretches of gorse and young bracken, but this was all the
better for Alexander's purpose for it meant that he could
follow the old woman without much risk of her noticing
it.

It meant also that there was plenty of cover for him to
bob down and hide in if she should happen to turn round
and look behind her, but he never had to do this for the
old woman kept looking straight ahead as she walked.

Mile after twisting mile went by like this. The going
became so rough that Alexander lost sight of the old
woman for minutes at a time, and even began to wonder
if he had wandered off the track altogether. Then he
would see it again, running faint but still recognizable,
through the grass and heather.

He began to tire. He was only ten, after all; it was
late in the afternoon and he had come a long way. Also,
he was a little frightened by this time for the path had
continued to lead upward for a long way. He could see
nothing but hills around him now and he knew he must
have come deep into the heart of the hill-country where
he had never been before.

"I'm lost!" he thought in sudden panic, and stood very
still and listened. No sound came to his ears. The air was
still and heavy, and there was a sense of thunder brood-
ing over the hills.

It was an eerie feeling standing there all by himself in
that lonely place, and for the first time since the tall
stranger's visit to the smithy, Alexander regretted his

refusal to wear Granma Thomson's charm. He would
have felt safer, much safer, with it round his neck now,
for now he was remembering certain things about the
hill-country and the people in it that he had forgotten to
take into account when he decided to follow the old
woman.

Yet still, he thought, it would be a pity to give up when
he had come so far, and for a few seconds more he stood
there, torn between his curiosity about the old woman
and the desire to run home as quickly as he could. Curiosity won, but only just. He took a dozen or so very un-
certain steps onward along the path, and stopped at a
point where it curved round a great stretch of rough,
dark gorse bushes.

Just at that moment, the thunder broke over the hills.
The gorse bushes swayed wildly. The prickly branches
beside him parted, and the old woman stepped out from
among them. She stood right in Alexander's path and he
stared at her, too astonished to say a word and too frightened to move so much as a finger.

FIVE

The Warning

"Do you know the danger you are in, boy?"

It was the old woman who spoke first—only, there was no point in calling her an old woman any longer for she was changing before Alexander's very eyes, and there was no doubt at all now that she was both young and beautiful.

The shawl she had worn round her head was gone, and the long hair falling about her shoulders gleamed black and sleek in the fading sunlight. Her eyes flashed dark and angry at him from a face as pale and delicate as white flowers in moonlight. The ragged old dress she had worn in the smithy was gone also, and in its place was a silken gown of the same light, soft green as the young bracken fronds uncurling at her feet.

When she drew herself up to speak, the silk of it rippled in graceful folds from a slender golden chain that clasped her waist. Alexander dropped his eyes from her face to the glittering chain and tried to answer, but between shock and fear he could not say a word.

"Speak, boy!" the woman commanded. "Do you know who I am?"

Alexander nodded. He knew who she was all right, but terror tied his tongue and he did not dare to name her for he was thinking that all the things he had heard about the hill-country must be true. There were fairy-people living there, he had been warned, and that was why neither he nor any other of the village children had ever been allowed to go there by themselves. The fairies would steal them away, they had been told, and keep them prisoner in their houses in the hollow hills.

And now here he was, alone and miles from home, with a fairy-woman standing right in front of him.

Slowly and fearfully he looked up at her again and this time, because he thought her eyes were not so angry as they had been at first, he found his voice again.

"You're one of *Them*," he whispered, still not daring to name her outright to her face, but when the fairy-woman only nodded to this, he took fresh courage from her silence. She hadn't done him any harm so far, he thought, and maybe she wasn't going to. More boldly now, he added:

"I knew ye were young when I saw ye at the smithy."

"I could see that," she answered, and frowned again.

"Then how was it my da didna ken?" Alexander asked

curiously. "Why should I see ye different from the way he saw you?"

"Because children see with the eyes of truth," she told him curtly, "and although we try to disguise ourselves from them as we do from grown people, we do not always succeed."

"Why did ye come to the smithy for a pot, then?" Alexander demanded. "Can ye no get anything ye want by magic, seein' ye are one o' *Them?*"

"Gold we have, and silver we have," said the fairy-woman, "and everything else we desire we can have by the power of magic—everything that is not made of iron. For we have no knowledge of working iron and so neither have we any magic that has power over it."

Alexander's spirits went soaring at this for he had imagined there was no limit to the power of the fairies. With the hint of a boast in his voice he remarked:

"My da would be a gey powerful man among such as you, then!"

The fairy-woman smiled at this, a small and secret smile, and she said softly:

"Aye, he would. All the more so since he has shown he has no fear of our ancient enemy, the warlock Hugo Gifford."

She looked at Alexander with a strange sly gleam in her dark eyes. "That is why I was sent to test whether his skill with iron is as great as it is said to be."

Alexander stared at her, not understanding why she

had made this last remark, and she went on in the same
soft, dreamy voice:

"Aye, the smith would have had a fine life among us,
sleeping soft on sweet moss at night and living merry in
the daytime. A week would have seemed but an hour to
him and a year with us would have passed like a day, for
we would have honored him like a prince for his skill and
made him rich, with silken clothes gentle against his skin
and fine gold chains to hang around his strong neck. He
would not have wearied of his captive state with all this
to content him."

And now Alexander understood fully what she meant.
It was not to order an iron pot she had come to the
smithy at first, nor was it to collect the pot that she had
returned to the smithy that day. It was as a spy on his father's skill she had come on her first visit, and it was as a
thief she had returned to steal him away with her to
work as a prisoner at making iron for the fairies.

As this dawned on him, he shrank back in terror from
the gleaming darkness of her eyes and stopped his ears
against the terrible things she was saying in that soft,
sweet voice. The fairy-woman frowned to see him do this
and, her voice now loud and harsh, she said:

"We know of the love your kind have for one another
although we cannot understand it. We would have put a
spell on him, once he was ours, to make him forget his
home."

"He would never forget! Never!" cried Alexander
wildly. "He would have been missin' my mam and Mag-

gie and me and Granma Thomson a' the time! And what would we have done without him?"

The very thought of this was enough to make the tears flow from his eyes and, sobbing, he went on:

"Ye hadna the right to make such a cruel plan against him—and him bein' kind to you and all, givin' you the pot for nothing because he thought ye were too poor to pay for it!"

"It's *you* should be grateful for his kindness," the fairy-woman said sharply, "for it was that and nothing else that saved him from my power this day."

Alexander looked up at her again, sniffing and rubbing his eyes. "How?" he asked. "How did it save him?"

"We must return good for good—that is our law," the fairy-woman told him. "A good deed from one of your people must be repaid by an equal kindness from us, and it was your father's kindness of heart, therefore, that forbade me to steal him away. For it is true that he would have been made unhappy by this until we could have thrown the spell of forgetfulness over him."

The thunder rolled again as she finished speaking, and as if the sound of it had reminded her of her first words to Alexander, she added:

"But your case is a different one. It was no kindness on your part to come peering and prying after me, and I have still to deal with that."

"Let me go, mistress," Alexander pleaded fearfully. "I meant no harm and it would break my da's heart if I didna come back safe to the smithy."

The fairy-woman looked at him thoughtfully, and there was a long silence.

"It may do more than break his heart," she said at last. "It may cost him his life if I do not let you return home."

She tapped her foot on the ground and glanced uncertainly around her as if trying to make up her mind about something. Alexander watched her anxiously, not daring to say a word in case that word would be the wrong one in the circumstances, and at last the fairy-woman seemed to come to a decision.

"Listen, boy," she said. "The smith has put us in his debt and we must repay him in full or suffer for it. Also, we have a common enemy in the warlock, Hugo Gifford, and there will come a day when the warlock will seek his revenge on your father for having crossed him. That is the time he will need to know what I am going to tell you now, so listen carefully and I will forgive your curiosity and let you go, for you are the only one who can take this message back to him. Are you listening?"

Alexander nodded his head. She closed her eyes and turned her face up to the sky, now rapidly darkening with the storm clouds rolling in over the hills. In a high, toneless voice she chanted softly:

Let silver bring who silver hath,
The silver shot shall bar the path.
Let silver cast who has the skill,

The silver shot shall bar the hill.
But a knot, a knot, two knots and three,
The storm-wife ties to raise the sea.

"Now repeat it," she ordered Alexander, opening her eyes again.

Once, twice, three times the fairy-woman made Alexander repeat the rhyme before she was satisfied he could say it all without stumbling over a word. Then she told him:

"Remember the warning I have given you, boy, and keep that rhyme fast in your memory. And when the time of great need arrives, tell it to your father."

"How shall I know when that time is?" Alexander asked, bewildered.

"It will be the time when the warlock strikes," the fairy-woman said, "and until then you must keep silent. Not a word must you tell till then of the warning I have given you, of the rhyme, or of seeing me as you see me now. If you do, our debt to the smith will be cancelled and we will be free again to try and win him for our own. Do you understand?"

It was all very clear and Alexander nodded to show that he did understand, although it seemed to him that he would burst if he had to keep such a secret from every single person he knew.

"See that you keep faith with me then," the fairy-woman told him grimly.

She raised an arm and pointed her long white hand along the path. "Now go—and do not look back. Otherwise . . ."

She left the warning unfinished, but she had still said quite enough for Alexander. He turned and ran, keeping his eyes on the path and straining to put as much distance as possible between himself and the fairy-woman.

The storm that had been gathering all the time he spoke to her broke as he ran. Thunder cracked like a giant's whip across the sky. The rain came pelting down and in a very few minutes he was drenched nearly to the skin. The long wet grass lashed across his legs and his feet slipped on the wet stones and the mud of the path, but still he kept running till he was back at the place where the fairy-woman had taken the pot from him and gone on alone.

Here he stopped to catch his breath and look around him. The path being clearly marked from this point and not so rough, he was now onto the easier part of his journey home. It was still raining hard, however. He was hungry for it was now long past his supper time, and he still had a good distance to go. However, there was nothing for it but to carry on, and so Alexander put his head down against the driving rain and trudged wearily forward.

The rhyme the fairy-woman had taught him ran round and round in his head all the time he walked, and he puzzled over its meaning. What was "silver shot"? he won-

dered. And who was the storm-wife? And when, he asked himself fearfully, would the warlock strike?

Question after question bubbled up in his brain but never an answer to any of them, and at last he gave up trying to puzzle out the mystery of the rhyme. He was too tired and miserable in any case to care after a while, and all he could think of was getting safely home and being warm and dry in his own safe, comfortable bed.

So he reached home that evening just when everyone was so anxious about him that his father was about to set off in search of him. His mother fussed over him, making him stand in front of the kitchen fire while he stripped off his wet clothes. Both she and his father asked him what had taken him so long to deliver the old woman's pot, and his mother said crossly:

"Ye should never have let the boy go a' that distance, Thomas."

"Ach, I wasna to know the auld wifie lived so far away," protested Thomas.

Alexander said nothing at all for he could see that both his father and mother had already decided on this explanation for his long absence. There was no need for him to add anything to it so far as they were concerned, but when he had finished his supper and gone up to bed, Granma Thomson came quietly upstairs and sat down beside him.

"Well, lad," she asked in a whisper, "what have ye up your sleeve that ye couldna tell your mam or your da?"

Alexander propped himself up on his elbow and said,

"It's a secret, Granma Thomson, and I've sworn no to tell a soul till the proper time comes."

"Dear me! Is it that serious?" she asked.

"Aye," Alexander told her solemnly. "It is."

"Well, well," said Granma Thomson. "Well, well!" And then she asked, "Would it be anyway concerned with the tall fellow that limped, this secret?"

"Aye," said Alexander. "It would."

"D'ye tell me that, now!" said she thoughtfully, and then she asked, "Have ye said your prayers, Alexander?"

"Aye," said Alexander. "I have."

"Here's another one for ye, then," she told him, "and it's a good one in the circumstances, maybe." And then she said:

From ghoulies and ghosties,
And long-leggity beasties,
And things that go bump in the night,
Good Lord, deliver us.   *Amen.*

Alexander gave a little laugh at this and said, "That's a queer one, Granma Thomson!"

"It's an old, old one," she told him. "A tried and true one, so just you say it now and say it again whenever ye're feared o' the warlock."

Alexander repeated the queer little prayer and then, when Granma Thomson rose to tuck the covers round him, he asked:

"What's a storm-wife, Granma Thomson?"

"Mercy on us!" she exclaimed. "What will the boy ask next?"

"I want to know," Alexander insisted sleepily.

"Well, there's one no very far from here," Granma Thomson told him. "She's an auld wifie that lives on the headland above the harbor down there on the coast of the Firth, and the fishermen ca' her the storm-wife because they say she can raise good winds or foul as she pleases by tyin' knots in a certain way in a piece o' twine."

"That's daft," Alexander argued. "How can she raise a wind like that?"

"Daft it may be," said Granma Thomson, "but the fishermen believe it. They even pay her to raise a good wind for them when their boats put out to sea, and I never yet knew the East Coast fisherman that would pay out good money for nothing!"

She bent over him and smoothed his hair. "Get you to sleep now, lad, and dinna worry about this secret o' yours till the proper time comes."

And so she left him to fall asleep, still wondering when *that* would be.

SIX

The Warlock's Wood

Alexander found it very hard to keep the secret of the fairy-woman's warning completely to himself, of course.

Time and again he was tempted to tell his father or Granma Thomson about it, but every time he opened his mouth to speak of it, he remembered the fairy-woman sternly telling him that to do so before the right time came would cancel her debt to his father and leave her free to try and steal him away again.

That was enough to make him shut his lips tightly again, and so the time wore on till spring was over, and still he had managed to keep the secret.

Summer came. The grass grew tall and green, with bright flowers twining their way upwards through it to the sun and fat golden bees bumbling their way into the honeyed hearts of the flowers. Alexander roamed in the woods with the rest of the village boys, picking wild strawberries, climbing trees, and sucking the honey from the purple shaggy heads of clover. He made tops and spun them, played "Run, sheep, run," "Leave-oh," and "Allie-over" all through the warm gold of the long summer days, and each evening when he came home to the cool, lavender-and-beeswax scent of the house, the memory of his meeting with the fairy-woman was fainter in his mind.

And so gradually it came to be that he only thought of it at all when he lay awake in bed at night with the moon shining silver-white onto his counterpane or a branch of the honeysuckle on the wall outside tapping long fingers against his window. Granma Thomson's queer little prayer was a great comfort to him at these times and so was the thought of the rowan wood hanging over the front door of the house. Alexander pinned his faith on both of these things when the fear of the warlock's revenge came into his mind, and so fell happily and dreamlessly to sleep.

It was a very peaceful summer for all of them, in fact, that year for Thomas kept to his resolve to do no more poaching in the Warlock's Wood. Janet's sharp tongue lost its edge when she found him staying home at nights and so knew she need not fear the shame of his being brought up before the Sheriff again. Granma Thomson stopped prophesying woe and doom to Thomas as the weeks slid by into months and still there was no sign of the tall stranger appearing to demand the trap he had left for repair. And when Thomas stopped telling his poaching yarns at the summer evening gatherings outside the smithy, the story of his trip to the Warlock's Wood was completely forgotten in the talk of other matters.

The minister remembered it, however, and every now and then he called at the smithy and reminded Thomas to be earnest in prayer and to attend church regularly.

"For that is the way to defeat the Powers of Darkness, Thomas," he advised. "Lay aside your poaching gear for the armor of righteousness, and they cannot touch you."

"Oh, I will, minister, I will," agreed Thomas.

To show that he meant what he said, he started going to church with Janet every Sunday, and while she stood small and neat in her best Sunday black beside his tall form, he bellowed out the Psalms of David loud enough to drown the choir.

"Hark at Thomas Thomson roaring away at the Psalms as if he had just this minute invented them himself," sniffed the rest of the village, taken aback at this sudden return of the black sheep to the fold. But Thomas didn't mind this for he had a good, tuneful voice and the Psalms of David were the best exercise he had found for it yet. And Janet, of course, was delighted at the change in his ways.

The laird was another one who remembered Thomas' story of his trip to the Warlock's Wood for, like the minister, he had been impressed by the strangeness of the tall man with the lame foot. He called in at the smithy one day and said to Thomas:

"Now look here, Thomas Thomson, you're a rascal and a poacher, but you're still one of my tenants and I've got a duty to see that no one interferes with you. So if you have any more trouble from that tall limping fellow, you're to call on me and I'll see that he's sent packing. The Sheriff will help, too. I told him about this visitor of yours and he agrees that the fellow sounds a bad lot and should be chased out of the county. D'you hear me?"

"Aye, laird, I hear you and I'm grateful for the offer," Thomas said. "But ye needna worry over yon fellow for he's never appeared again. His carriage is still there in the shed where I put it after the wheel was mended."

"Well, he'll likely leave you alone for good if you leave off poaching in his wood," the laird told him.

"Oh, I will, laird. I will," Thomas agreed.

He meant what he said to the laird also, of course, but that was high summer when the hunting season was dead anyway. It was when summer was past and harvest time over, too, that he began to think differently.

The old fever to be out and about in the woods by night came over him then so that sometimes he would rise quietly from his bed and stand at the window in the moonlight watching for the sight of a hare's big ears standing up black against the stubble of the cornfields, or listening for the harsh call of a pheasant from the woods. And without admitting the reason for it to himself, he began to spend odd hours working on his traps till they were all in good repair.

It was always after the rest of the household was in bed that he did this, and it was on one of these occasions that the longing became too strong for him and he slipped out once again to poach in the Warlock's Wood.

It was a perfect night for poaching—just enough light for him to see what he was doing and yet dark enough for his movements to go unnoticed. He trod cautiously through the wood, keeping his distance from the warlock's castle this time, and setting his traps with all the noiseless skill of his practiced hand.

The wood was very quiet, too quiet really for his liking, for there was something rather eerie about the silence. However, nothing happened to disturb him or to frighten the mare, Peggy, and he had good luck with his traps that night.

Delighted with himself, he gathered all the spoils together and set off for home, but he had not ridden very far when he was struck by a thought that caused him to pull Peggy to a sudden halt.

How could he explain his bag of game to Janet? Or to Alexander? Or to Granma Thomson?

Alexander would be worried if he knew his father had been to the Warlock's Wood again, and as for the two women——! Thomas groaned aloud at the thought of what *they* would say. He wouldn't have a dog's life with the two of them nagging at him, he thought mournfully, and sat there considering ways and means of getting out of the trouble he had brought on himself.

For a while he could think of nothing; then suddenly there came into his head an idea so comical that he nearly exploded with laughter. Chuckling, he kicked his heels against Peggy's flanks and turned her head in the direction of a village that lay a few miles east of his own. Quickly and quietly on her padded hoofs she trotted toward it, and just before dawn they were there.

Thomas dismounted then and hid Peggy in a clump of trees just beside the nearest house. Still chuckling to himself, he crept silently up to the back door of the house and dropped a hare on the doorstep. Over the garden wall he went then to the house next door, and left a pheasant lying there for the owner to find in the morning.

So he worked his way from house to house, leaving a hare on one doorstep, a pheasant on another, and a brace of rabbits on yet another until he had disposed of his whole bag for the night. When he was finished, he ran silently back to where Peggy waited, and rode quickly home bubbling over with laughter at the thought of the expressions on the faces of the people who would find his mysterious presents.

In the smithy stable, he untied the padding from Peggy's hoofs, crept quietly into the house, and tiptoed upstairs. Janet never stirred as he slipped into bed, and when she woke an hour or so later, he was snoring peace-

fully away like the good, law-abiding husband she thought he was.

It was too good a joke not to be repeated, Thomas thought to himself when he woke in his turn. And forbye, the more people who found these unexpected gifts at their back doors, the more the mystery would deepen and the more fun he would get out of hearing all the talk and discussion about it.

Of course, it would be a sacrifice of the good meals he might have had himself out of his night's bag, but he wouldn't have enjoyed these anyway with Janet nagging at him. It would be far funnier and certainly far wiser to rid himself of the evidence in this way, he decided, for if he did, he could go poaching to his heart's content and nobody would be upset.

Three nights later, accordingly, Thomas was up to his tricks again. Already, by this time, he had heard amazed talk and all sorts of wild guesses as to where the first lot of game had come from, and on his way home from the second expedition, he left the various things at a different lot of houses from the first ones.

The gossip about the mysterious appearance of this second lot of game and the guesses about where it had come from spread quickly to his own village, and everyone there had some theory to air on the mystery. It was a madman was behind it, said some, and others said no, it was some rich man doing good to the poor by stealth. There were others who thought it must be witches' work and that it would be dangerous to eat the things, but nobody got anywhere near the truth for Thomas had taken great care not to be seen and, so far as the village knew, he was still leading the life of a reformed character.

Not a hint of the real state of affairs did he let drop to a soul. Even when he was aching inside with laughter at the wild guesses that were made at the evening gatherings in the smithy, he managed to keep a straight face, and even put forward a few theories of his own—just to keep the pot boiling, so to speak.

It went hard with him, of course, not to be able to share the joke with Alexander and Granma Thomson. However, he had to accept that sharing the joke with them would mean the end both of it and of his poaching and, dearly as he would have liked to laugh over it with them, he still managed to keep the joke to himself.

So for many a week in the autumn of that year the matter remained a mystery, for every few nights during this time Thomas made a trip to the Warlock's Wood, and each morning on his way home he left the results of his night's poaching for various astonished householders to find at their back doors.

He always had a good bag for there was plenty of game in the Warlock's Wood, and nothing else happened to frighten him or Peggy the way the owls and the broken trap had done on his first trip. He came across some strange things, however, the like of which he had never seen in his life before.

Once, when he was fishing one of the pools in the

small trout river running through the wood, his line was caught by a tangle of weeds overhanging the bank. The current whipped it right into the ripple of water beneath the overhang. Thomas lay down flat on his stomach and groped under the weeds to find it again, and his fingers touched something cold and hard. The line was wound round this thing and he pulled them both up together, laid them on the bank, and had a look at the cause of the trouble.

It was a figure shaped out of clay—a little manikin about four inches long and partly crumbled away with the flowing action of the water.

Thomas' fingers were shaking as he unwound his line from it for he knew what it was and he knew why it had been put in the river. A witch, he had been told, would make a clay figure of some person she wished to harm. Then she would put it in the running water of a stream, and as the action of the water crumbled it away, so would the person waste away with the sickness she had wished on him.

There was only one way to break such a spell and that was to destroy the figure before the action of the water had caused it to crumble away completely. Thomas thought of this as he rose to his feet and stood looking at the little manikin lying on the grass and, in a sudden rush of rage at the witch who had made the spell, he stamped it to pieces.

"That'll teach them!" he said aloud, but his voice sounded odd and lonely in the night silence, and when he went back to fishing again it was with many an uneasy glance over his shoulder.

There were other charms he discovered, usually when he was digging away the earth to bury the wire of a snare at a point where two paths crossed. This was a good place to set a snare and it was also a favorite spot for a witch to place a spell, but after he found the manikin in the river, Thomas never stopped to examine these other spells or to wonder what their purpose was. It was enough for him that they were evil things and that he would break their power by destroying them.

This he did, with great satisfaction at the time, and it was only after the deed was done that he sometimes felt uneasy at having interfered with the witches' work.

He was not afraid for himself, of course, otherwise he would never have been there in the first place. But suppose the witches revenged themselves on Alexander, or baby Maggie, or Granma Thomson—or even Janet?

Thomas felt guilty when he thought like this, but after all, he told himself, all four of them were safe inside the house with the rowan wood over the door when he was out at night. Maggie had the double safeguard of her coral charm, and through the day, of course, he would be there himself to protect them all. And he was alert to all the witches' tricks. They would never get past him!

As for his promises to the minister and the laird——! Well, thought Thomas to himself with a shamefaced grin, his promises about poaching had always been like piecrust—just made to be broken. However, so long as he continued to be cautious, no one would be any the wiser of that, so why worry?

Now Thomas was quite right to suppose he had covered his tracks well and, in fact, it was only pure accident in the long run that led to at least one person discovering what he was up to.

That person was Alexander, who happened to wake up one night with a raging thirst caused by the salt herrings he had eaten for supper. It was no use trying to go to sleep again until he had had a drink of water, Alexander decided, and so he slipped out of bed and crept quietly down to the kitchen.

He was reaching up to a shelf for a cup when he suddenly noticed that his father's traps were not in their usual place on the hooks driven into the wall below this shelf. He was still sleepy, so that it was a moment or two before he realized what this meant. Then, as he stood staring at the empty hooks, he heard a sound from outside the house. It was the rattle of the bolts on the stable door that he heard, and then he understood.

His father was going poaching, and that very minute he must be bringing Peggy out of her stable!

Alexander ran to the kitchen window and peered out. He saw nothing at first and, of course, he didn't hear Peggy stepping on her padded hoofs through the smithy yard. A moment or two later, however, she passed the window with his father on her back. Alexander watched to see whether she would turn to the right, which would mean that his father was off to the laird's estate. To his dismay, however, his father turned the mare's head to the left and Alexander realized that he must be making for the Warlock's Wood.

He would have shouted after Thomas but the words stuck in his dry throat. Barefooted as he was, he would have run after him, but his feet seemed to be rooted suddenly to the cold stone of the kitchen floor. And by the time the spell thrown by the shock of the moment had passed, Thomas was out of sight and the opportunity to stop him was over also.

In a daze, Alexander wandered over to the fire, and crouching down beside the few red embers in the grate, he thought of the fairy-woman's warning that the warlock would have revenge on his father.

It was quite an effort to recall everything she had said for it all seemed so long ago to him now, and he had had so much to think about since then. He had almost forgotten the words of the rhyme she had taught him, in fact, but now as he sat thinking of the danger his father might be in, he remembered them exactly.

And yet, he thought despairingly, he daren't tell them to his father—not till the warlock actually struck against him, or he would be in just as great a danger from the fairy-woman! What was he to do?

It was cold sitting there and Alexander was both puzzled and afraid, yet still he was unwilling to go back to bed. He would not sleep anyway, he thought, till he saw his father safely home again. Moreover, if he waited downstairs for him, he could catch him as he came back from the stable in the morning and, without his mother overhearing, beg him not to carry on taking the fearful risk of poaching in the Warlock's Wood.

And so Alexander settled down to wait for the morning and his father's return home. He put his head down on his knees and said Granma Thomson's little prayer to himself, and then just sat there, shivering occasionally because it was so cold and he was still afraid.

An hour ticked by on the kitchen clock. Alexander's eyes began to droop shut. He jerked them open and inched nearer to the dying fire, hugging his knees in an effort to get warm. The clock slowly marked off another hour. The embers in the fire faded into black cinders and Alexander's head began to nod. His eyes drooped shut again, and before he realized what was happening to him he had fallen asleep on the hearth rug.

He was still lying curled up there when Thomas came quietly into the kitchen on the following morning. Puzzled by this sight, Thomas bent down and gently woke him, but Alexander was so dazed at first that he could say nothing except:

"Oh, Da, ye shouldna have gone to the Warlock's Wood again—I was feared for ye, Da, I was awful feared!"

Thomas held him close to comfort him, and when he felt how Alexander was trembling with cold and fear, he was ashamed of himself for being the cause of it.

"Poor laddie," he said. "Did ye wait the whole night for me, then?"

"I had to wait. I had to warn ye," Alexander said through chattering teeth.

"There was nae need, laddie. I ken the risks," Thomas tried to reassure him, but Alexander cried wildly:

"No them a', Da! Ye dinna ken them a'!"

He drew a deep breath as he made up his mind to tell his father all about the fairy-woman, but he never had to do so for Thomas took one look at his white and frightened face and before he could speak again said gently:

"Come to bed, son, and sleep, for your troubles are over. I promise ye I'll never poach the Warlock's Wood again!"

With that, he lifted Alexander up in his arms, carried him upstairs to bed, and put a hot brick at his feet to warm them. As he tucked the covers round him he said:

"I'll swear to that on my own anvil, Alexander, and that's a promise no smith can break. So ye see, ye'll never have to worry or keep watch for me again!"

Alexander smiled up at him, content, and Thomas left him to sleep, knowing that this was one promise he could never break for never again could he risk bringing such fear and unhappiness on his own son.

Later that day, accordingly, he did swear on his own anvil, with Alexander watching him, that he would never poach the Warlock's Wood again. The two of them were well pleased with this little ceremony and they went back into the house together, Thomas feeling that he had done his best to make amends for the trouble he had caused and Alexander with his mind at peace at last.

However, the damage had been done by that time. It was too late now for promises, too late to try and avert the warlock's revenge for laming him in the trap and for the breaking of the spells the witches had set in the wood —too late for anything. And although neither Thomas nor Alexander realized it then, they very quickly found out that this was the situation.

SEVEN

The Silver Shot

It was only two days later that the tall stranger who had called himself H. Gifford, rode up to the smithy on his black horse and demanded the trap which had been left to have its wheel repaired.

As bad luck would have it, Thomas was away at the time, returning a pair of the Sheriff's carriage horses that he had just been shoeing. Alexander was alone in the smithy, and the first thing he knew about the stranger's presence was his mother appearing in the doorway with baby Maggie in her arms and telling him to come and harness up the trap the gentleman had left for repair.

Alexander's bones froze to the very marrow as he realized what she meant, and remembered also that she knew nothing of their suspicions about the tall stranger. He tried desperately to think what his father would have done in the same position, but between his fear and his mother urging him to hurry up, he could think of nothing.

Slowly he came out of the smithy. The tall stranger was standing in the yard watching him and Janet with a grim half-smile on his narrow face, and Alexander circled cautiously past him to the door of the shed where his father had put the trap. It was quite light and easy for him to pull out and, once the stranger had quietened the horse's restlessness with the same strange words as before, he had no difficulty either in harnessing it—he being well used to helping with such work in the smithy.

Not a word was spoken in all the time it took to do this—not even by Janet, who usually had plenty to say for herself, and at last Alexander found courage to whisper to her out of the corner out of his mouth:

"Yon's a bad lot, Mam. Get you into the house away from him—quick!"

Janet gave him a look that was puzzled and more than a little frightened.

"I dinna like the look o' him, right enough," she whispered, "but I canna leave you, son."

The stranger watched their whispering with the sneering half-smile still on his face; then he took a step toward Janet. She backed away from him. He took another step, and another, with Janet backing from him all the time, and then he reached out a hand to her. Janet screamed, and just as she did so, Granma Thomson chanced to appear round the corner of the smithy.

"Run, Alexander!" Granma yelled, her sharp old eyes

taking in the situation at a glance. "Run for your da, quick!"

Her voice broke the spell that held both Janet and Alexander. Janet whipped round and almost threw baby Maggie into Granma's arms, and then she braced herself in front of the pair of them with her own arms spread out as if to protect them. And, as Maggie passed from one to the other of the women, Alexander took to his heels and ran from the yard at the top of his bent.

A glance behind him as he ran showed him Granma Thomson hobbling with Maggie to the safety of the house, and his mother struggling in the grip of the tall stranger as he forced her into the trap. The sight put spurs into Alexander and he ran like the wind toward the Sheriff's house.

There was no difficulty about finding his father there. He was standing on the drive leading up to the house, talking to the Sheriff. The laird was there, too, and the three of them were laughing and joking away like the best of friends while the carriage horses Thomas had just returned cropped the grass beside the drive. Their laughter stopped like a tap being turned off, however, at the sight of Alexander and the tears staining his face. Thomas caught hold of him as he blundered to a halt and gasped out:

"The warlock, Da! He's taken Mam away in his trap!"

Thomas gaped at him, dumb-struck with astonishment and dismay. Then with a roar of anger, he swept Alexander up into his arms, threw him across the back of one of the carriage horses, and leaped astride it behind him. The laird and the Sheriff were nearly as quick at mounting the other horse, and double-mounted like this, the four of them thundered down the drive and along the path to the village street.

Doors flew open on either side of the street as they came clattering down it, and by the time they reached the smithy, there was an excited trail of men, women, and children streaming after them, all shouting and asking one another the cause of the excitement.

Granma Thomson was waiting for them in the smithy yard, but the trap was gone and of the tall stranger and Janet there was no sign. Thomas slid down from his horse, bringing Alexander with him, and shouted to Granma:

"Where are they? Where has he taken Janet?"

"Where *would* he take her but to his own Goblin Ha', ye donnert great ass!" Granma screamed back at him. And then her anger gave way to tears and she sobbed:

"Poor Janet! Poor lassie! If she had only held onto the bairn, the charm round its neck would have guarded her too. But she tried to save it! She gave the bairn to me to hold and took a' the danger on herself. Oh, she was brave —brave, the poor lassie!"

Thomas beat his fists against his head in despair. "He warned me himself something like this would happen if I crossed him again," he cried. "The warlock warned me! *'When will you be needin' the trap again?'* I asked, and

'*That depends on yourself,*' he told me—but I was too blind to see the threat in his words!"

"Ye great gowk!" Granma Thomson screamed. "Did you go poachin' his wood again?"

"Aye, many times. And broke some of his witches' spells forbye," Thomas confessed miserably.

"Oh, heaven forgive you for a bad son and a worse husband, for I might but Janet never will," Granma moaned.

The Sheriff came up on one side of Thomas at this and the laird on the other. The minister appeared from somewhere out of the crowd and began to comfort Granma Thomson, and the Sheriff told her:

"Enough of this weeping now, mistress. If some bad character has stolen Mistress Janet away, I'll have the law on him and we'll soon have her back."

"First you must catch him, Sheriff," the laird said grimly. "Have you any plan that will catch Hugo Gifford, the warlock?"

And while the Sheriff scratched his head over the answer to that puzzler, the news passed in whispers from mouth to mouth that it was Hugo Gifford who had stolen the smith's wife. The minister broke into this whispering with another question:

"Are you remembering what day this is, good people?"

None of the grown people in the crowd grasped what he meant at first, but all the children there shouted immediately:

"*It's Hallowe'en!*"

Some of them began to prance about pretending to be witches on broomsticks while others laughed and cheered them on. Thomas and the laird stared at one another in even greater dismay than before.

"Hallowe'en," Thomas whispered, "——the night of all the year when the witches' power is at its strongest! That's why he has delayed his revenge till now!"

"I'll call all the men together and we'll go into the smithy," the laird told him. "We'll have peace there to decide what must be done."

Thomas nodded and walked off toward the smithy. Alexander ran after him, tugging at his coat-tails and crying:

"Wait, Da, wait! I've something to tell you!"

"Tell it in the smithy," Thomas threw over his shoulder.

The men crowded through the smithy door after him and he faced them, standing with his back to the forge. Alexander danced with impatience in front of him.

"*Listen*, Da! I've a message I was to give you come the time of the warlock's revenge."

Thomas seized his shoulder and held him still. "A message? What message?"

"It was the old woman that got the iron pot from you," Alexander told him. "She tried to stop me seeing where she lived when I carried it home for her, but I followed her and she turned out to be one of—*Them*."

"A fairy-woman?" one of the men asked, smiling and thinking this was just some childish fancy of Alexander's.

He laughed and so did more of the men when Alexander nodded and said:

"Aye, she was a fairy-woman, right enough."

Thomas hushed the men down. "There *was* something gey queer about that old wifie," he told them. "I couldna think what it was at the time, but . . . Go on, son. What happened?"

"She said Hugo Gifford would have his revenge on you but he was the enemy of her people too, and you had been kind to her and so she would tell me how to save you. But I wasn't to tell you till the proper time came or she would steal you away to make iron for the fairies like she had meant to do in the first place before you put the debt of your kindness on her. Then she gave me a message for you."

Alexander paused for breath because he had rattled all this out as quickly as he could. Thomas bent eagerly toward him.

"Quick, son! Tell me the message!"

Everyone leaned forward the better to hear, even the men who had laughed, and in a clear voice Alexander recited:

Let silver bring who silver hath,
The silver shot shall bar the path.
Let silver cast who has the skill,
The silver shot shall bar the hill.
But a knot, a knot, two knots and three,
The storm-wife ties to raise the sea.

Thomas straightened up and so did everyone else, looking at one another in bewilderment as they tried to unravel the meaning of the rhyme, but it was Thomas himself who struck the first clue for he suddenly remembered the three paths leading to the Goblin Ha'.

"I have it!" he cried. "The rhyme is a warning to bar the three paths to the Goblin Ha'—the one from the town, the one from the hill-country, and the one from the sea!"

Alexander tugged at his coat-tails again. "Why, Da? Why?"

"It's Hallowe'en, remember," one of the men said with a scared backward glance over his shoulder into the shadows of the smithy. "They say that all the warlocks and witches in Scotland ride every year to the Goblin Ha' to celebrate Hallowe'en with Hugo Gifford."

"So it is not only Hugo Gifford we will have to deal with tonight," Thomas groaned. "It is every other witch and warlock in the country as well. Oh, Janet—my poor Janet! What will they do to her!"

"Bear up, Thomas. We will bar the paths to them as it says in the rhyme," the Sheriff said. "But first we must think how to do it. How *can* we stop the witches in their tracks?"

"The rhyme has the answer to that too, Sheriff," the laird said slowly. "*Silver shot!* That's the only thing will stop a witch in her tracks—a silver bullet!"

"*Let silver bring who silver hath,*" the minister muttered. "I see it now! Those of us who have silver must bring it to be melted down into silver bullets!"

And Thomas, with sudden hope in his voice exclaimed, *"Let silver cast who has the skill*—that means myself! I am the only one here with enough skill in metals to cast bullets out of the silver!"

"There's the last bit of the rhyme, too," Alexander reminded him, "the bit about the storm-wife."

Granma Thomson came pushing her way through the men, calling out, "Aye, and now I ken why Alexander here was askin' me what a storm-wife was! *A knot, a knot, two knots and three*—that's the very order of knots the old storm-wife at the headland ties to raise a foul wind off the land that will blow ships out to sea! We must get her to do that for us, Thomas. We must raise the sea against the witches that mean to come by boat and then take the sea track up to the Goblin Ha'!"

"Aye, we'll do that too," Thomas agreed. "We'll do all that the fairy-woman said must be done."

"You can have my silver, Thomas—every scrap of it!" the laird offered eagerly.

"And mine!" the minister cried. "I'm off to fetch it now!"

"I'm off, too, Thomas!" the Sheriff shouted. "I'll be back soon with every bit of silver I can lay my hands on!"

Thomas threw off his jacket and snatched his leather apron from its hook on the wall.

"Get the fire started in the forge!" he roared. "Bring in that wood from the yard. Fetch your tools, carpenter, and start making the frames for the bullet molds. Bring out the biggest iron vat in the smithy—a ladle for pouring the silver into the molds—tongs—ramrods—every gun in the village——"

Like bullets themselves his orders came shooting out. Everyone scattered to obey, and within minutes the smithy was humming with a dozen different activities.

The village carpenter fetched saw and plane and vise, and set a team of men onto making the wooden molds for shaping the bullets. Men carried in great loads of fuel for the fire, and two of the strongest men pumped the bellows till they had the biggest fire the forge had ever seen blazing there. As the silver arrived—plate, candlesticks, christening mugs, and vases of all shapes and sizes, other men threw it into a great iron vat and hoisted this onto the fire. Men cleaned guns, checked the size of the bore, and called it out to other men who listed it and passed it on to the mold-makers.

Alexander darted hither and thither, lending a hand whenever one was called for, running errands from one man to another, and greatly enjoying the excitement of all this grand plan to rescue his mother. No one stopped to eat as the hours slipped by. There was no time for that, but Granma Thomson brought in a tray with beer for the men and milk for Alexander and a dish of cold meat, and they all snatched mouthfuls of this as they worked.

Thomas was at the center of all the activity, stirring the molten silver, ladling it out from the vat, and pouring it from the ladle into the molds; plunging the hot bullets into tanks of water to cool them, and then passing them as fit to be fired from the guns.

The laird and the Sheriff issued the finished bullets to each man and checked his gun, and at last everything was finished and they were ready to go. It was dusk outside now and so there was no time to waste, for as soon as darkness fell the witches were certain to be on their way to meet with the warlock at the Goblin Ha'.

EIGHT

The Storm-Wife

"Now this will be the order of things," Thomas told them all. "You will divide yourselves up into three parties—so —one led by the laird, one by the Sheriff and one by the minister."

He went among them dividing them up into three groups and hushing down the questions the laird and the Sheriff started to ask.

"Laird, will you lead your group to the hill road?" he asked, and the laird said he would.

"And you, Sheriff, will you take the guard on the path to the town?"

"I'll do that, Thomas," the Sheriff agreed.

Thomas turned to the minister. "Reverend Goudie, I want you to take the sea path and guard it from the headland where you can see any ship that stands in to the harbor. You will be handy there also to the storm-wife's house."

"I'll willingly lead the party to guard the sea path," the minister said, "but someone else will have to ask the storm-wife to raise a foul wind, for you know that a man of my calling is not allowed to do such a thing."

"Ease your mind, minister," Thomas said tartly, "for I wouldn't ask it of you! Alexander will go with you and speak all that has to be spoken to the storm-wife."

"Whatever you wish, Thomas," the minister said. "The boy can ride on my crupper."

Thomas fished in his pocket and handed over some money to Alexander. "You'll have to pay the storm-wife, son," he said. "Ye ken what to say to her, now—eh?"

Alexander took the money and nodded, "Aye, Da."

"That's settled then." Thomas looked round the three groups of men all standing ready with their guns loaded with silver bullets. "You had better make a start now."

"Not so fast, Thomas!"

The laird and the Sheriff both spoke together; then they stopped and looked at one another and it was clear that it was the same question that was troubling them— the one Thomas had brushed aside a few moments earlier. The Sheriff nodded to the laird, and he spoke again for both of them.

"What are *you* going to be doing, Thomas, while we bar the three paths to the witches?"

Thomas looked at him with a long, sober look. "Ye've forgotten Hugo Gifford, laird," he said slowly at last.

"There's only one man here has the duty to tackle him, and that man is myself. I'm going straight to the Goblin Ha'."

"Alone?" the laird asked, astonished, and Thomas nodded, "Aye. Alone."

"But you'll go armed, surely?" the Sheriff objected, looking at Thomas' empty hands.

Thomas shook his head. "If Hugo Gifford could have been killed by a silver bullet, he would have been dead long since. No, Sheriff, I'll take no gun with me for I have a better weapon than that to use against the warlock."

"I think I can guess what you are driving at, Thomas," the minister said quietly.

Thomas turned to him. "Aye, minister, you read your Bible more than the rest of us so maybe you *can* guess— but it's only a guess, mark you!"

"Tell us what you mean, Da!" Alexander cried, for he had listened in terror as his father said he would face Hugo Gifford alone and now he could bear the suspense no longer.

"I'll tell you part of it," Thomas said, "and the whole of it I'll tell you on the day you become a smith like myself. As for these others, lad, they can only ever know the part I will tell now."

He looked slowly round them all, and then he picked up his great fourteen-pound hammer and he said:

"I'm a smith by trade, my friends, and I'm a master of my craft. The man who taught me was a master in metal also and he, in his turn, was taught his craft by a master smith. And so on, right back through the ages to the days of Tubal-Cain—the man who is named in the Book of Genesis in the Bible as the first of the world's workers in metal. Everything that a smith must know to become a master of his craft was first taught by Tubal-Cain. And Tubal-Cain was taught by God."

Everyone in the smithy was deathly still and silent, for never in their lives before had they heard such serious words from Thomas or seen such an air of authority as rested on him now. With all their eyes fixed on him and everyone listening intently for his next words, Thomas went on:

"So God gave Tubal-Cain the secrets of working metal and made him a master of the craft. And besides this, He gave also to Tubal-Cain a Word of Power that could only be passed on to each man who became, in his turn, a master of the smith's craft. That Word of Power is known to me, therefore. And so this—!"

He swung the hammer in his hand up into the air and held it high above his head, and they all looked up at it.

"—this is my weapon against the warlock! My smith's hammer and the Word of Power God gave to Tubal-Cain!"

No one spoke as Thomas brought the hammer down again and stood leaning on it. The silence lasted for a long moment, and was broken at last only by the shuffle of feet as the men moved forward one by one to shake Thomas by the hand and mutter a "God-speed" to him.

Quickly then they filed out of the smithy. The horses they would ride had been fetched earlier and left tied up at the mounting block by the door, but there was not enough of them for each man to have a mount. Some rode double-mounted, some grasped a stirrup and ran beside another man's mount, and like this they clattered off down the village street to the point where they had to separate to cut across country to their different guard points.

Alexander rode on the crupper of the minister's horse and Thomas edged the mare, Peggy, up to him at the moment of parting.

"Do your part well, my son," he said gently, "and I'll bring your mother back, safe and sound."

With this, he turned Peggy's head again and set out on his lonely road to the Goblin Ha'.

"Hold tight, Alexander," the Reverend Goudie said. He put his horse to the trot and they were off toward the sea road and the headland where the storm-wife stayed.

Now the last of the short daylight of late autumn was gone and they were riding through the plum-colored darkness of the last night in October. Alexander held tight with both hands gripping the broad leather belt round the minister's middle and peered ahead, but all he could make out was vague shapes of trees and hedges and the road slipping past under the horse's hoofs like a dark ribbon unwinding.

He smelled the sea before he saw it, and shortly after the first sniff of salt, seaweedy air reached him, he saw a grayish blur ahead. The gray blur took on a steely shimmer. The minister pointed to it and said in a low voice:

"There's the sea, Alexander. It's always lighter over the sea at night because the water reflects the stars, and so we will easily see the witch-ship standing in to the bay."

The ground began to rise up in a gentle slope, and Alexander guessed they were climbing toward the headland. The slope grew steeper and the going became harder for both horses and men for the ground they trod on was uneven, scattered with sandy hollows and broken by rabbit holes that caused many a stumble.

"We're nearly there!" The Reverend Goudie turned in his saddle and called encouragingly to the men behind. "Look, Alexander!"

He pointed forward to the top of the headland, and on the flat ground there Alexander saw the squat dark outline of the storm-wife's house. There was a light in the window. The minister stopped his horse beside it and called to the men to go forward to the edge of the headland.

"I'll stay outside here in case you need me," he told Alexander.

"I'll no need anyone, minister. I ken what to say," Alexander said confidently, but in spite of that his knees still shook a bit when he came to knock on the door of the house for he had never seen a storm-wife before and he had no idea what to expect.

A voice called him to come in. He pushed open the little low door of the house and stepped straight into the storm-wife's kitchen.

It was small and gloomy. The only light in it came from the red glow of the fire in the grate and from the wick burning in a little stone lamp filled with oil. The storm-wife sat in a rocking chair just beside this lamp and Alexander could see that she was old—older than Granma Thomson even, but there was none of Granma Thomson's lively expression about her wrinkled brown face. It was as still and expressionless as a piece of carved wood. Only the sharp little eyes darting a knowing look at him seemed alive as he held out the money his father had given him and said:

"My name is Alexander, mistress; son of Thomas Thomson the smith, and I am come to pay you for the raising of a foul wind off the land that will blow a ship full of witches out to sea and stop them harming my mother at their Hallowe'en revels."

The storm-wife gave a cackle of laughter at this and began to rise slowly from her chair.

"Eh, that was a pretty speech," she said in her cracked, old-woman's voice. "And how d'ye ken I can do this, my braw young lad?"

"I ken fine ye can," Alexander said boldly, "for I was first told to ask it of ye by one of *Them*. 'A knot, a knot, two knots and three' she said you would tie to raise a storm."

"Aye, aye, that's the proper spell," the storm-wife said approvingly.

She made a sudden grab at the money Alexander was holding out to her and then hobbled over to the fireplace with it and put it in a jug on the mantelpiece. Then she lifted a big black kettle off the hob, poked the fire up, and set the kettle on top of the blaze.

"The kettle, the kettle must sing for the storm too," she muttered to herself, and then she took down from a hook in the wall beside the fireplace a long piece of blackish string.

"A knot, a knot," she muttered, and her twisted brown fingers began tying a knot in one end of the string. Round and in and out and round and below and suddenly crosswise she passed the string through her fingers, and now there was a curious-looking knot at one end of it. Another knot the same she tied some distance from the first one, and then she looked at Alexander and cackled again.

"Now, there's the fair wind out of the west safely tied up," said she in a satisfied voice.

The twisted old fingers began twisting in and out of the string again. Alexander watched them closely to see how she would tie the two knots and then the three, but he was soon confused by all the strange turns she gave to the string.

"What wind have you tied up now?" he asked when the two knots were finished.

"The fair wind out of the east," she told him, "and now I'll tie up the fair wind out of the north with three knots, and after that you'll come outside with me while I let loose the foul wind out of the south!"

Her fingers went back to twisting the string and by the time the three knots were tied the kettle on the fire had begun to boil. A soft whistling sound came with the feather of steam rising from its spout, and the storm-wife glanced at it with another approving cackle.

"We can go now, my fine young sir," she told Alexander. "It's time to whistle up the foul wind out of the south."

She picked up a black shawl lying over her rocking chair and put it over her head. Then she pushed the knotted string into her apron pocket and shuffled to the door. Alexander followed her and stepped outside, wondering what was going to happen next. The minister was waiting for him a few yards off, still mounted on his horse, and when the two of them came out he called:

"Is all well with you, Alexander?"

"Aye, sir. All's well," Alexander called back.

The storm-wife took no notice of either of them but hobbled steadily on toward the edge of the headland. Alexander followed a few yards behind her and the minister came on behind him. The men waiting on the headland drew back at the storm-wife's approach but she paid no attention to them either.

She went straight to the very edge of the turf, and turning her back on the cliffs dropping below it with the sea washing round the foot of them, she faced inland to the south and began to whistle.

It was a long shrill whistle on two notes she gave and the sound of it was so strange and piercing that it sent a shiver down Alexander's back. Three times she whistled, long and shrill on the two notes, and then she stood with her head cocked as if she was listening. She muttered something and then calling out, "Ye'll get the foul wind ye paid for, young sir," she shuffled back to her house, cackling and muttering to herself.

The minister dismounted and stood beside Alexander. The rest of the men drew in around them and they all stood peering out to sea, watching for the witches' ship.

Up there on the headland, the wind was cold. It whistled round their ears, making them all shiver, and suddenly one of the men said:

"The wind's changed!"

He wetted a finger and held it up. "It's true—the wind's swung round to the south!"

A little murmur ran round the rest of the men. Alexander hugged himself and said in an awed voice:

"It was the storm-wife did it. *She* brought the foul wind out of the south!"

"We'll need it!" the minister broke into his words. "There's a ship standing in. Look there!"

He pointed out to sea and one by one they made out the lines of a ship, sails spread and making for the bay below them.

The wind from the south grew suddenly stronger.

"Listen!" whispered one of the men. "It's the witches' ship all right. Can ye hear them?"

Alexander peered toward the ship, listening hard. There were lights bobbing about on its deck now, and faintly through the sound of the rising wind he heard laughter and wild shrill music coming from it.

The wind from the south was still mounting, churning up the sea into huge waves that dashed and broke with a roar against the rocks below the headland, whipping through the men's hair and blowing their jackets about them. Alexander felt himself stagger under the force of it and the minister threw an arm over his shoulders to steady him.

"It's blowin' a gale now, sir, a real gale!" Alexander shouted exultantly.

"Aye, they'll not make landfall against this if it keeps up!" the minister shouted back.

The lights on the ship were swinging wildly about as if the people who carried them were running to and fro in panic, and now it was screams of terror instead of laughter that came from the ship. The wind rose to its full fury. The ship heeled over and sails went flapping loose from its spars. Now it was no longer driving into the bay but being blown out to the open sea again, and now also there was real danger of those on the headland being blown over the cliff by the terrible force of the wind hurtling off the land.

The men crouched down, holding on to one another. The minister kept his grip on Alexander, and peering out from under the shelter of his arm, Alexander watched intently as the witch-ship was finally driven out to sea and lost forever in darkness and a fearful wilderness of stormy water.

When it was all over at last, those on the headland turned away and mounted their horses for the journey back to the smithy. Not a word was spoken among the men as they rode for they were all too awed by the terrible fate that had overtaken the witches to have any heart for idle chatter about it. And as for Alexander, seated once more on the crupper of the minister's horse, his mind was too full of the peril facing his father and mother to have room for any further rejoicing over his own success with the storm-wife.

So they rode home in silence to the smithy where Granma Thomson had the kettle simmering on the hob for them. She made tea for them all, and they sat round the fire drinking it while they told her about the fate of the witch-ship and waited for the return of the Sheriff and the laird from their part in stopping the witches.

Twice Alexander fell asleep in his chair and jerked awake again before these two returned, for they were a long time in coming. When they did arrive, however, they had good news to tell so that he was glad he had not crept upstairs to bed as he had felt like doing several times while he waited for them. The laird began the story, standing in front of the fire with his coat-tails up to warm himself while he spoke.

"The Sheriff and I started off by arranging what we

would do," he said, "once he had come face to face with
the witches from the town and I had met those coming
down from the hill. We decided we would hold both lots
up at the point of our guns, and then give them the choice
of a silver bullet through the heart there and then or of
riding quietly with us to be locked up in the county jail."

Granma Thomson cackled with laughter. "It wasna
much of a choice!'

"It was not," agreed the laird, "and I, for my part, had
no difficulty in persuading the witches from the hill to
come quietly to the jail with me."

"The witches from the town were no harder to per-
suade once such a stern choice had been put to them,"
said the Sheriff, "and I was not much behind the laird in
getting them under lock and key."

"What will ye do with them now, sir?" Alexander
asked. "Ye surely canna let them loose to frighten us
again once *this* trouble's over!"

"Never fear for that, my lad," the Sheriff told him.
"The whole lot of the witches in the jail will come up
before me in court tomorrow, and I'll put an end to their
cantrips then, I can tell you, for I'll sentence every last
one of them to be banished the country!"

"There willna be a witch or warlock left in Scotland
then!" cried Alexander, and the minister said thank-
fully:

"Good riddance!"

Everyone began to laugh at that until they remembered there was still the most powerful warlock of all to

deal with and that they had no idea yet of how Thomas' part in the night's work had gone. The laughter died away then, and they all continued to sit around the fire looking as serious and fearful as they felt.

NINE

Thomas and the Warlock

Thomas had farther to ride than the minister and Alexander's party, and the wind the storm-wife had raised struck him just as he reached the unsheltered stretch of moorland he would have to cross before he entered the Warlock's Wood.

He welcomed the sudden onset of the storm, however, for it told him that Alexander had managed to buy the foul wind from the storm-wife, and so with the hope in his heart that the laird and the Sheriff would be equally successful, he buffeted his way forward across the moor and into the wood.

To his surprise when he got there, he found that the path by which he had chosen to enter it was was overgrown with brambles, and he was puzzled by this for he had remembered it as being perfectly clear and open. He had no choice but to turn round and take another way into the wood, but when he had ridden a little way along this second path of his choice, he was dismayed to find the ground becoming so marshy under Peggy's hoofs that she was in danger of sinking right into it.

Hurriedly he dismounted and led the mare back to firm ground, wondering all the time why it was that he had never come across that particular piece of boggy ground in the wood before.

A third time he chose a path, and this one did not lead into bog nor was it blocked by brambles. It was lined on either side, however, by small birch trees with long, thin branches that stretched out over it at the level of his face, and flicked against him as he rode like so many whips.

The stinging blows of these branches were hard to endure, and Thomas was just about to dismount and lead Peggy, when she shuddered and reared back from something lying on the path. Her movement was so sudden and Thomas' mind was so distracted at the time that he was taken completely by surprise. The reins flew out of his grasp, he fell forward on Peggy's neck and tumbled toward the ground.

As he fell, he saw the thing that had startled Peggy. It was an adder, and its poisonous, diamond-patterned head was raised to strike at him. Just in time he saw it, and just in time his hand shot out and the hammer gripped in it came down on the snake's head.

Thomas scrambled to his feet and looked at the dead snake. He was a man of the countryside and he knew that adders were attracted to dry banks and sunny places, not to dark, wet woods. Moreover, he was perfectly certain that none of the three paths he had tried had been blocked before in the way they were now.

There was no doubt about it, he thought. It was all the warlock's work—no doubt meant to delay him till the witches were all gathered at the Goblin Ha' and the Hallowe'en revels could begin.

Well, if the laird and the Sheriff were as successful as Alexander and the minister had been, there would be no witches at the Goblin Ha' that night. And come what might, he would find a way through the wood. But he would have to leave Peggy where she was and trust to luck that she came to no harm, for it was quite clearly going to be impossible to ride her past the kind of obstacles that were being put in his way.

Once decided on this, Thomas lost no more time. He looped the mare's reins round the stump of a tree and went on on foot, his hammer ready in his hand for whatever he might encounter. And so began a very nightmare of a journey.

The wood seemed to have been changed completely from the one Thomas had come to know so well. Paths that he had never seen before crisscrossed before him in a maze of tracks, all of which led only into bog or into thickets of brier and bramble. Strange and horrible-looking growths leaned forward to cut at him with spiny stems or to wrap long and clinging tendrils about him. Unseen and unsuspected, pits opened out beneath his feet and dropped him into clumps of nettles, man-high, that blistered his face and hands with the stings from their coarse green leaves.

Yet, still undaunted, Thomas plunged on. With his hammer, he crushed down the clawing stems of the brambles and brier. With his bare hands he tore away the clinging vines from his legs, fought the nettles clear from his face, and climbed out of the pits. He smashed branches from trees to pave a safe way for himself over the bogs. And with his countryman's keen sense of direction and his poacher's eye for the lay of the land, he kept on the right track for the Goblin Ha'—and Janet.

Like most easy-going men, he had a terrible temper when roused, and by the time he had worked his way nearly to the outer edge of the wood, his grief at having Janet snatched from him and his remorse at having delivered her into the warlock's hands by his own folly had all been turned to a great and raging fury against Hugo Gifford.

When he strode out of the farther side of the wood at last, therefore, he was an awesome figure—a big, hard-breathing man, his clothes torn to rags and his face all scratched and bleeding, but with his hammer held high and ready and the muscles of his great arms swelling with the vengeful strength that was in them.

The bleak ruins of the outer walls of the castle showed no movement, but at the top of the central tower the sentinel owls were ready. Harshly screeching, they swooped down on Thomas. He beat them off with his hammer as he ran, and more than one fell to the strokes he gave before he reached the safety of the inner walls where they could not follow.

Edging along these walls then, he stepped through an archway and found himself in the roofless remains of a fair-sized room. The owls were circling overhead and quickly he worked his way round the walls of this room till he came to a stone stairway that led downward.

For a dozen steps or so, he trod cautiously down, and now he found himself in a large room with a great stone-vaulted ceiling and stone walls richly hung with tapestries. There were no windows in the room, but it was plentifully lit with candles in tall golden brackets fixed to the stone walls. There were no furnishings apart from these, and it looked to Thomas like a great ballroom from which all the dancers had fled, leaving it haunted with the knowledge of the strange event that had driven them away.

Another stone stairway spiraled down from a corner of this hall, and this led Thomas down to yet another level of the tower. This one held a maze of small rooms, some lit, some in darkness, none of them furnished, and all, it seemed to him, holding this ghostly feeling of something suddenly happening and of people fleeing that mysterious moment of terror.

Down he went from this level, and down again from room to room and level to level, feeling now that he must be the only living creature in this place of vanished life. But somewhere, he knew, he must find Janet and the warlock himself in the castle, and it must be soon for now he was well down into the underground part of the tower, and so he must be near the warlock's own demon-built chamber.

An archway opened ahead of him with light coming toward him through it. Thomas gripped his hammer firmly and stepped through the archway into the light and into the warlock's underground cavern.

Hewn out of the solid rock it was, just as he had heard tell it would be, and carved on the smooth black stone of the walls were the signs of the zodiac and other mysterious symbols of the warlock's magical power. The signs danced and flickered at him in the candle gleam that lit the chamber, and the black stone of the walls glowed with the red reflection of the flames in a great fireplace at its farther end.

Hugo Gifford himself stood in front of this fireplace, with Janet crouched weeping at his feet. His tall form was still clothed all in black, but instead of the dress of an elegant gentleman, he now wore a long black robe, a black cloak that swept down from his shoulders to the ground, and a conical black hat on his head.

As Thomas appeared in the doorway, he lifted his right arm, pointing one long hand toward him, and before either Thomas or Janet could cry out at the sight of one another, a blaze of fire sprang up where the warlock had pointed.

The fire made a wall ten feet deep that stretched from

side to side of the demon chamber, the flames of it leaping roof-high and blazing with a fierce red heat in front of Thomas' face. Above the sound of their crackling, he heard Janet cry out to him and looked wildly for a way to reach her, but there was no way except through that wall of searing fire.

"Fire is the tool of the smith," Thomas argued desperately to himself. "I have worked with fire, borne the heat of it all my manhood days—I cannot let the fear of it conquer me now!"

And throwing his leather apron up over his head to protect at least his face from burning, he plunged forward into the roaring heart of the flames.

The heat snatched his breath from him. He gasped, choked, and staggered blindly to keep his footing. The fire tore at him, laying the agony of burning on the bare flesh of his arms. His eyes streaming tears of pain, his mouth open in a roar of protest against it, he blundered on. And still roaring aloud with the torture of his burns, he emerged at last on the other side of the wall of fire.

In the same instant, the fire vanished as if it had never been. Only the burns on his arms remained as proof of the ordeal he had come through, and the flames that still licked from his clothes.

In a daze, still half-blinded with the tears of pain smarting in his eyes, Thomas beat furiously at his smoldering clothes. He stumbled forward to snatch Janet from her crouching position at the warlock's feet. She ran to meet him, crying out with relief to see him still alive, but the warlock's pointing finger shot out at her and she was brought up short in her tracks.

Thomas seized her reaching hands, but could not budge her from the spot where she stood. He dropped his hammer, gripped Janet round the waist and tried to lift her but still, for all his strength, he could not budge her from the floor. She was stuck to it as fast as if her feet had become a part of the rock from which the demons had carved it so long ago.

"Help me, Thomas! Help me!" Janet screamed, clutching him round the neck. Yet sweat and strain as he would to lift this little woman only half his own weight, Thomas could not move her so much as an inch.

The warlock chuckled at the sight they made, and the more Thomas tried to lift Janet, the more he laughed. The black rock walls echoed his laughter and sent it bouncing and rolling back and forth through the underground chamber until it seemed to Thomas like the laughter of a thousand demons cackling in his ears. Janet's shrieking and sobbing added to the din, and at last Thomas could stand it no longer. He let go of Janet and bawled:

"Wheesht! Wheesht, woman, and let me think!"

"The warlock's told me what ye've been up to," Janet screamed at him. "Ye should have thought before ye went poachin' in his wood! Ye should have thought before ye lamed him in yon trap! Ye should have thought before ye broke the spells ye found in the wood!"

"Aye, Thomas, ye should have thought. Ye should have thought!" the warlock echoed in a mocking imitation of Janet's voice.

"I didna mean this to happen, Janet!" Thomas cried despairingly. "I love ye, woman—I wouldna have ye harmed for the world!"

"A fine love that brings me to this pass!" Janet screamed. "I rue the day I married ye, Thomas Thomson!"

"A fine love, Thomas! She rues the day, she rues the day!" Hugo Gifford echoed in the same tones, and it was this second piece of mockery that gave him away, for it let Thomas understand suddenly how the warlock was managing to hold Janet fast there.

It was nothing more than her own spite at himself the warlock was using to hold her! Poor Janet—she was on the same side as Hugo Gifford's evil will, so long as she was holding anger in her heart at his foolishness, and that was why the warlock was able to hold her fast in his power!

"Forgive me, Janet!" Thomas cried out as soon as he realized this. "Oh, say ye forgive me!"

"How can I forgive such bad ways as yours," sobbed Janet, "when *this* is what happens because of them?"

Still Thomas begged her, " Janet, Janet, true love forgives all. Say ye love me truly, lass. Say ye forgive me, before it's too late."

The warlock's laughter stopped as he spoke, and the sudden silence was far more terrifying than his laughter had been. The anger in Janet's face turned to fear again at the silencing of the warlock's laughter, and she looked up at Thomas with tears spilling out of her eyes.

"I'm feared, Thomas," she said pitifully. "I'm feared o' yon terrible great black warlock and what he means with me."

Thomas put both his arms round her. "Say ye forgive me then, Janet, say it and mean it with all your heart," he pleaded, "for there's nae warlock can harm true love."

"She's mine! She's mine, smith," the warlock cried harshly, "for hers is no true love."

"It is! It is!" Thomas roared, and Janet turned her head over her shoulder and flashed out at the warlock with all her old spirit:

"Hold your wheesht, Hugo Gifford! I'm no yours *yet!*"

And then, for all her brave words still thinking she was a doomed woman, poor Janet turned to look at Thomas again. Such a face of despair was on him then that a great tenderness for him came over her and she was suddenly ashamed of the anger she had been holding against him.

"Ach, I ken ye didna mean me harm," she said, her voice all weak and trembling with the feeling that was in her, "and for the sake of the true love I bear ye, Thomas lad, I *do* forgive ye the faults that brought me here."

With a shout of triumph at these words from Janet, Thomas pulled her sharply toward himself, and light as a feather now she came into his arms. Over her shoulder he saw the warlock advancing on them, snarling with rage at this second defeat, and swiftly picking up his hammer from where he had dropped it in the struggle to free Janet, he backed away. Holding Janet close he cried: "Ye have no power that will hold us apart now, warlock!"

"Be brave, Janet. He has no power against true love," Thomas whispered. Janet clung to him without a whimper and the warlock cried——

——But no! The words he spoke cannot be retold here for it would burn the tongue to speak them and deafen the ears of those who heard such a force of magic.

All that can be told of this moment is that a loud rumbling noise followed on the sound of the warlock's voice. The noise came from behind Thomas and Janet. They whirled round to face it and stood thunderstruck at the sight that met their eyes.

The walls of the Goblin Ha' were in motion all round them, all the solid rock of it shivering and rumbling and shaking as it moved inward to close the gap of the archway that formed its only entrance. Both Thomas and Janet stood frozen with terror and astonishment at their first sight of the moving walls, and by the time Thomas recovered his senses it was too late.

"Quickly!" he yelled, and on the word swept Janet with him to the last little crack remaining of the space where the entrance had been, but it closed just as he threw himself against it.

"We're trapped!" Janet gasped, her eyes traveling

round the now smooth, unbroken surface of the rock walls enclosing them.

"Not yet!"

Thomas pulled her behind him, spat on his hands, and hefted his blacksmith's hammer. High above his head he raised it, great shoulders opened wide, the muscles of his arms tensed to their utmost. The warlock rushed toward him, both arms upraised and his mouth open to utter a spell that would stop the blow descending, but before the words could leave his mouth, Thomas had brought his hammer driving down with the full force of his great strength against the wall of the demon chamber. And as his hammer struck ringingly against the stone, he called out the Word of Power God gave to Tubal-Cain.

On the sound of that Word, the warlock screamed in agony and stopped his ears with his hands, the wall split jaggedly like a tree riven apart by lightning, and as the crack in it widened, the warlock dropped, still writhing with agony, to the floor.

The crack in the wall split suddenly wider and became a gaping hole, and all round it other cracks appeared and the rock began to tumble.

"Run for it!" Thomas yelled, seized Janet by the hand and pulled her with him through the hole. No sooner were they both through than the rock collapsed behind them. Crash after crash followed as the walls of the demon chamber caved in, and with the whole building shaking around them, they scrambled up from the under-

ground level and through all the floors above it till they reached the outer walls.

No owls lay in wait there now—"Not now the warlock is buried under the stones of his own demon chamber!" Thomas thought grimly. The wood held only the familiar patterns of the paths he had come to knew so well, and Peggy was waiting patiently where he had left her to carry them both safely home to the smithy.

When Alexander saw his mother standing at the kitchen door there at last, he flew out of his chair like an arrow leaving a bow and was into her arms before she could even open her mouth to say:

"I'm home!"

Janet hugged Alexander, and then Granma and baby Maggie. Thomas hugged them all together, and then shook hands with the laird and the minister and all the men. And when he had told his story and they all knew what fate had befallen Hugo Gifford, Alexander said:

"Well, now we *can* say 'good riddance!' "

"Good riddance!" cried everybody, and this time there was nothing to stop them laughing!

And that is the whole story of why there are no witches or warlocks any more in Scotland. Or so they say, anyway, and they might very well be right for certainly there has been no sign of any of them again from that day to this. Which is just as well, all things considered!